AN ENGLISH TRAGEDY IN GREECE

The sun was dropping now, fiery above the columns of the Propylaea. Patrick saw Miss Amelia standing still to gaze back at the great mass of the huge entrance. The accident happened in a flash; the youth knocked into Miss Amelia as he hurried past her, and with arms outstretched to grab helplessly at the air the frail figure of the old schoolmistress arched outwards, struck the landing at the foot of the drop and rolled over, bowling down to end in a sprawling heap at the foot of the stairs. Miss Amelia Brinton was quite dead. Her faded eyes stared sightlessly up at the Grecian sky, and there was no vestige of any archaic smile on the mouth that was stretched in the shocked rictus of sudden death.

GRAVE MATTERS

MARGARET YORKE

BANTAM BOOKS
TORONTO · NEW YORK · LONDON · SYDNEY

Note:
All the characters in this story are imaginary
and bear no relation to living persons

*This low-priced Bantam Book
has been completely reset in a type face
designed for easy reading, and was printed
from new plates. It contains the complete
text of the original hard-cover edition.*
NOT ONE WORD HAS BEEN OMITTED.

GRAVE MATTERS

*A Bantam Book / published by arrangement
with the Author*

PRINTING HISTORY

First published by Geoffrey Bles 1973

Bantam edition / January 1983

ISBN 0-553-22914-1

Published simultaneously in the United States and Canada

Bantam Books are published by Bantam Books, Inc. Its trademark, consisting of the words "Bantam Books" and the portrayal of a rooster is Registered in U.S. Patent and Trademark Office and in other countries. Marca Registrada. Bantam Books, Inc., 666 Fifth Avenue, New York, New York 10103.

PRINTED IN THE UNITED STATES OF AMERICA

H 0987654321

To my brother
John Larminie
with love

PART ONE

Miss Brinton paused before the row of maidens who supported the temple's portico roof on their heads. She gazed at each one of them in turn. Dr. Patrick Grant, Fellow of St. Mark's College, Oxford, seated nearby on a broken marble pillar also contemplating the Caryatids, watched her, and wondered if she, too, deplored the fake. In the bright light that shone from the sinking sun, her five sisters seemed to glow with a mellowness denied to her. He could hear a guide telling a group of tourists in bitter tones about the removal to England of the original. Many of Greece's ancient treasures would have been lost for ever without the interest of foreign archaeologists, he reflected. He stood up and looked to the west, where the great columns of the Propylaea stood out against the sky. He had come up to the Acropolis this evening to watch the sun setting behind the great entrance monument. There was still a little time to wait, so he wandered off in the direction of the museum, behind the Parthenon.

Miss Amelia Brinton was bound for the museum too; she walked ahead of him, paying no heed to the flocks of tourists with their shepherd guides and clicking cameras, an erect, white-haired figure carrying a faded green and white woven bag, relic of a much earlier visit to Greece.

Patrick had first noticed her a few days before, at Delphi. She had been sitting halfway up the theatre with a small volume on her lap, sometimes reading it, and sometimes looking down at the stage, her head tilted, as though she were listening. There was something familiar about her, and later, when he saw her walking slowly down from the temple of Apollo in her sensible rubber-soled shoes, her linen hat in her hand, he realised where he had seen her face before: a portrait of those strong features had hung in the hall of the school which his sister Jane had attended; she had been the most forceful headmistress of its history, ruling over it for fifteen years and retiring just before Jane went there. Ever since, legends about her reign had been handed down to succeeding generations of pupils, and Miss Amelia herself had appeared in person on Speech Days and other such celebrations. She must be nearly eighty now. Patrick had not spoken to her at Delphi, and he had not seen her again until today. He remembered that she was the daughter of E. C. Brinton, a celebrated classical scholar in his day.

He watched her in the museum. She clearly knew it well, and paused before particular exhibits as though greeting old friends, unaware of anyone around her. Patrick's own appreciation of the past was often interrupted by his interest in the present, and his attention wandered now from the archaic smiles of the charming Korai to the equally archaic responding expression on the face of the old woman looking at them. Then he got sidetracked by the strange, three-bodied *daemon* with its bearded faces still bearing traces of colour that had once been vivid, and he forgot about her, until he realised that the museum was about to close and he was almost the last to leave.

The sun was dropping now, fiery above the columns of the Propylaea. Patrick walked slowly up the steps at the eastern end of the Parthenon, into the great space within, and emerged on the northern side, facing the Erechtheum once again. He stayed there for a while, watching the sun as it sank lower and lower. The crowds had thinned out, and against the light one could not easily distinguish individuals. He did not see Miss Amelia Brinton until he had passed through the columns of the Propylaea; then he recognised her below him. Beside the marble, glowing golden in the light of the sinking sun, the moving human figures on the stairway looked insignificant. Everyone walked slowly. A few people were still coming upwards, for the Acropolis did not close until the sun had fully set. Patrick saw Miss Amelia standing still to gaze back at the great mass of the huge entrance. She had paused on a transverse slope with her back to a steep drop above a long, straight flight of steps. She was right at the edge: if she were to lose her balance, or step backwards, she might slip over. With an urgent sense of impending disaster Patrick began to hurry down towards her. At first he did not notice a youth who was hurrying upwards, elbowing his way through a cluster of people on the lowest steps. The accident happened in a flash: the youth knocked into Miss Amelia as he hurried past her; Patrick saw the long, dark hair, and the slight figure in jeans and an open battledress jacket as the boy thrust on upwards heedless of the old lady. There was a little scream, repressed because even in the ultimate experience the training of a lifetime is not swiftly cast aside, and with arms outstretched to grab helplessly at the air the frail figure of the old schoolmistress arched outwards, struck the landing at the foot of the drop and rolled over, bowling down to end in a sprawling heap at the foot of the stairs. No one caught her. No one broke her fall. Patrick raced down the stairs himself, to arrive beside the crumpled little heap just as a horrified Greek tourist policeman was pulling down the grey skirt to cover the thin thighs that had been so crudely exposed. Miss Amelia Brinton was quite dead. Her faded eyes stared sightlessly up at the Grecian sky, and there was no vestige of any archaic smile on the mouth that was stretched in the shocked rictus of sudden death.

Patrick was not wearing a jacket, but he had a clean handkerchief in his shirt pocket. He bent, closed the staring eyes, and covered up the wrinkled face. Someone brought down the woven shoulder bag which Miss Amelia had dropped as she fell. Someone else brought the worn pigskin purse which had fallen from it, and a small leather-bound volume. It was Euripides' *Alcestis* in the original Greek, Patrick noticed as he replaced it in the bag. Maybe that was what she had been reading up at Delphi, hearing in her mind what must have been to her familiar words.

The whole incident ended in minutes. The Greek police were extremely efficient, swiftly guiding away from the body all the appalled witnesses who were exclaiming excitedly in several languages. A stretcher appeared as if by magic, and the sad little corpse, wrapped in a blanket, was soon decently concealed behind the ticket office, waiting for an ambulance. Only then did Patrick remember the heedless youth who had gone thrusting upwards through the crowd to cause the tragedy.

"It was an accident, *kirie*. The *kiria* was old and slipped," Patrick heard the Greek policeman who seemed to be in charge saying anxiously.

"Yes," Patrick agreed.

"She was your mother?" the Greek was asking, with concern.

"No," Patrick said. "The *kiria* had no sons."

"*Po, po, po*." The Greek tossed his head in sympathy at such a serious misfortune.

"I will go with the *kiria*," Patrick said. "But first—that young man who hurried past her—it was his fault. He knocked against the *kiria*." Patrick looked upwards at the mass of the Acropolis, gold now in the fading light. The Greek policeman followed his gaze.

"The Acropolis is closed now, *kirie*. There is no one up there," he said.

"I suppose you're right." Patrick still scrutinised the hill. Later tonight the monuments would be picked out in brilliant floodlights, while thousands of people watched the spectacle of *Son et Lumière*. He walked away from the little group of officials and climbed the steps once more. Apart from himself, there were only a few policemen making sure that all the tourists had, in fact, gone. There was no trace of any long-haired youth in jeans. He must have left with the last stragglers, and there would be no way of finding him. He could have been Italian, British, French—any nationality, even Greek, though few young Greeks wore their hair so long. He might even have been quite unaware of his responsibility for the accident.

A patch of white caught Patrick's eye in a cleft between the rocks. He picked up and saw that it was a page from Benn's *Blue Guide to Athens and Environs*, jaggedly torn from its binding. Patrick looked at it for a moment; then he folded it carefully and put it in his wallet. After that he went back down the steps.

"I must telephone the British Embassy," he said.

"But certainly, *kirie*." The Greek officials were thankful that the poor dead *kiria* at least was not alone. Though not her son, the English *kirios* was clearly her friend, and a man of authority who would take charge of things on her behalf.

After making his telephone call, Patrick followed Miss Amelia in a taxi to the mortuary. There, he witnessed the listing of what was in her woven woollen bag—a few drachmas in her purse, some boiled sweets, a grey woollen cardigan, and the small leather-bound *Alcestis* he had seen before.

II

"And I suppose you went to the funeral?" Patrick's sister asked him. They were in his set at St. Mark's, where Jane had come to lunch before a dental appointment in Oxford. They had eaten cold beef and salad, and now Jane was sitting on the window seat in his room while she drank her coffee. Below, in the Fellow's garden, two middle-aged dons were engaged in their fierce daily croquet duel. "Was anyone else there?"

"A chap from the Embassy and the proprietor of the hotel where she was staying. And the undertaker's men hovered around."

"How bleak," said Jane.

"It was, a bit. When the Embassy realised who she was—E. C. Brinton's daughter, I mean, as much as the esteemed former headmistress of Slade House, they gave her the full works—service in St. Pauls, with Bach and Elgar on the organ, though of course no hymns, since there was no congregation. It was all done very correctly."

"Hadn't she any relations?"

"She had a niece. The hotel man knew about her, because Miss Amelia stayed there every year and had told him. He said she used always to come with another old lady, a Miss Forrest, but she has a bad heart now and wouldn't come this year."

"I suppose it would have cost a lot for the niece to fly out."

"No one could get hold of her. She was out of England herself—on holiday too, probably. So the Embassy carried on. In that climate you can't delay. It seems they often have to cope with this sort of thing, when Britons die alone in foreign spots. I can think of many worse places to leave one's bones in than Athens."

"Is there a British cemetery? There must be."

"There's a Protestant section in the main cemetery. It's divided from the main part by low walls, and there's a gate from it to the road—the chaplain disappeared through there after the service, instead of processing back through the rest of the cemetery. It took about ten minutes to walk from the gates to the grave."

"How awful!"

"It wasn't, really. It's an incredible place, the cemetery. Immense, with huge, ornate monuments in the Greek part, some with photographs of the dead person in little shrines. There are lots of priests around—you know, the *papas* in their tall black hats with their beards and their hair in buns. And widows. So many widows, all in black, some quite young. A Greek widow wears black for the rest of her life," Patrick said. "And they weep. They show their grief in other countries. It's only in Britain that this stiff upper lip stuff goes on. Nearly every other nation displays emotion."

Jane looked at her brother for a moment.

"You're a great one for displaying it yourself, of course," she said, with irony.

"One conforms, in one's fashion," Patrick said.

"I suppose you've written all this to Miss Amelia's niece? About the funeral, I mean?"

"Er—well, yes. Even if she doesn't care a hoot, I thought she should know it was all properly done," Patrick said.

"You're a funny old thing, aren't you?" Jane said. She looked round his elegantly furnished room. Three oars were suspended high upon one wall, above a pair of impressionistic paintings by an artist in whose future Patrick had faith.

"Why?"

"So tough, you'd like us all to think. But inside you're a veritable marshmallow."

"You mean because I went to Miss Amelia's funeral and then wrote to her niece? You'd have done the same."

"Yes, but I'm a female. We do these things."

Patrick felt obliged to defend himself from this charge of sentimentalism.

"The niece had a right to know the details. And I was able to tell her that her aunt had died instantly—she can't have known a thing."

"There wasn't any trouble over that?"

"No. It would have been quite impossible to trace that feckless youth, just as you can't catch the demon driver who cuts in and causes two other cars to have an accident while he disappears, scot-free."

"Have you heard from the niece?"

"Valerie Brinton? Yes—just a rather formal note of thanks. She would have heard from the Embassy too, of course."

"Valerie Brinton," Jane mused. "She didn't go to Slade House. I think her parents lived abroad, I remember her being talked about. And I do remember Miss Forrest. She was there in my time—little and ancient, it seemed even then. She taught art. It must be the same one. She retired while I was there. Old Amelia had a country cottage somewhere."

"Near Winchester," said Patrick. "Valerie Brinton wrote from there. A village called Meldsmead."

"I suppose Miss Amelia left her the cottage. How nice for her."

"I suppose she did."

"Well, it's time I left for my appointment with the torturer," said Jane. "I'll just wash first."

She went through the door that led into his large, comfortable bedroom, off which opened a landing with a tiny kitchenette installed where once there had been a cupboard. At the far end of his bedroom a door disclosed his private bathroom. No wonder Patrick couldn't be bothered to marry, she thought, as she often did when she visited him here. Everything was laid on for him; he had a scout to minister to his daily wants; good food provided to the accompaniment of first-class conversation and even, on gala occasions, eaten off gold plate that had been bequeathed to the college by a long-dead former member; and spacious accommodation in part of the original college building. At least he hadn't embarked on croquet yet, though. She looked out of his bedroom window and saw the two combatants below, still warring. They were a chemist and a sociologist who sincerely hated one another and fought each other over matters of college politics whenever they got the chance, as well as joining battle of any kind that offered. Jane feared that Patrick might get like this as he grew older, and she was sighing over this problem when she rejoined him.

"What a sad sound," he said. "Do you dread the drill?"

"No," Jane answered. "I'm sighing over you. Even if there exists upon this earth a woman who would put up with your ways, how could she compete with all this?" She waved her hand around, gesturing at the high ceiling of his large room, the cornice decorated with elaborate plaster-work. "You're much too comfortable as you are."

"You're right, my dear. I am, and I don't plan to change a thing," Patrick said. He kissed her. "Can you find your way down? I'm expecting a pupil any minute. Mind he doesn't barge into you, he won't see you coming through his tangled mane."

"Oh dear," said Jane. "How can you bear it?"

"He's got terrible acne, poor boy. Perhaps it's better not to have to look at all those pimples."

"They might go if he washed the matted locks," Jane pointed out.

"He'll clean himself up soon and face the world, when he feels a bit braver," Patrick said. "He's a nice lad. Very bright, but rather insecure."

"Aren't we all?" Jane said. Even you, in your way, she thought. "Thanks for lunch. Come and see us soon."

She went away, and it was only as she entered the

dentist's waiting room ten minutes later that she realised because it was still the vacation, Patrick's pupil must be coming to consult him about some problem, not for a tutorial.

III

Among the Fellows of St. Mark's was a venerable don who lived in honourable retirement in a tiny cottage owned by the college. Once a year he visited an equally ancient Canon who lived in rather similar circumstances in Winchester, except that he had a wife who, though bent with rheumatism, was still able to cook and administer the household. The two old men had been friends from youth. Dr. Wilmot's sight was very poor now, and no one thought it safe for him to make his annual pilgrimage by public transport any longer, so Patrick drove him down to Winchester on the Saturday after Jane's visit.

It was a lovely morning in late September when they left Oxford, with the sun gilding the leaves that still clung to the trees. The harvest had been early, and the farmers were well ahead with their ploughing; there were still some fields of bleached or burnt stubble standing, but in most of them the rich, dark earth had been turned up in neat furrows. For a while they talked about a new building in a corner of the college grounds. Dr. Wilmot deplored the modern architecture of its design, but Patrick felt one could not ape the old. This discussion kept them going happily for half an hour until the old man suddenly fell asleep; Patrick drove on, enjoying the scenery in silence. Some way south of Newbury he noticed, on a straight stretch of road, a signpost pointing to the left which read *Meldsmead 2 miles*. Meldsmead was the village where Miss Amelia Brinton had lived, and from which her niece had written to him.

Dr. Wilmot woke suddenly and carried on at once with the conversation they had been having from the point where they had left it. Patrick, who had been mentally back in Greece reviewing Miss Amelia's fatal fall, had some trouble in returning his thoughts to plate glass windows.

He delivered his passenger and remained for a glass of sherry with Canon Fosdyke and his wife; then, despite pressing invitations to share their cottage pie, he left. He would call at a pub somewhere on the way back and have a sandwich.

It was such a lovely day that he felt reluctant to stop, and drove past several likely places. Then he realised that he was near the turning to Meldsmead. It was only ten past one; there must be a pub in the village. He felt curious to see where Miss Amelia had spent her retirement; somehow he would have expected her to choose a spot handy for the British Museum or the London Library, not a remote Hampshire village. He slowed down to watch for the sign, and soon came to it. After he had turned off the main road he found himself in a narrow lane with high hedges on each side; it was twisty, and he went slowly, for there was not much space to pass if he met another car. He passed a farmhouse and a few cottages before he reached the village, and at a bend in the road a red mini came hurtling much too fast towards him. The side of the Rover brushed against the hedge as he pulled in to give it room to dash past. He had time to see that it was driven by a woman with auburn hair, but no more; then it was gone, scattering dust behind it as he saw in his mirror. He drove on, even more slowly than before, but met no one else, and was soon in Meldsmead. The main road, such as it was, straggled through the village, with two turnings off to the right, each saying *No Through Road*. Another, to the left, led on to further villages, according to a signpost. There were more houses further on, but The Meldsmead Arms was at the junction of the main road and the first of the dead-ends, so Patrick stopped there. He would have a beer and a snack, and look round the village afterwards.

There were several cars parked outside the pub, and the public bar was very busy. He went into the saloon bar, where his entrance caused very little interest. Three youngish-middle-aged couples, the men in polo-necked sweaters and the wives in smart trouser suits, sat at a table talking hard and barely glanced at him. They were discussing some trip by boat they planned for the next day, and Patrick, eavesdropping as he drank his beer, gathered that one of the couples owned some sort of yacht or cabin cruiser.

The publican was a large man with an almost totally bald head and a small, neatly trimmed moustache. Patrick mentally labelled him an ex-serviceman; he discovered later, in fact, that Fred Brown was a retired regimental sergeant-major. The girl helping him behind the bar was obviously his daughter. Despite an unruly mop of dark brown curls she looked exactly like him.

The sailing group were talking about tides. Patrick drank his beer and listened to them. The boat seemed to be moored somewhere in the Solent. Besides them, there was a trio of men at the window all talking together. Patrick was too far away to hear what interested them, but soon one of them came to the bar to order another round for all three, and while he waited asked Patrick if he were just passing through.

"We don't get many casual callers," he explained. "Eh, Fred?"

Fred, behind the counter, agreed, with some regret, Patrick thought.

"We do well when there's racing at Newbury, though," he allowed. "People think it's worth turning off the main road then."

"Yours the Rover TC?" Patrick's new acquaintance enquired.

"Yes." Patrick knew very well that it was the only strange car drawn up outside the pub.

"Hm. Nice car. Wish I could run one. I have to use a pick-up for the market-garden. My wife has a mini. We use that on smart occasions."

"A red one?" Patrick asked, warily.

"No, mustard-coloured. Why? Did you meet a red one in the lane?"

"Yes." Patrick said no more but drank deeply from his tankard.

"Going rather fast, eh?" said the other man, and Patrick nodded. His new friend chuckled.

"She's not a real native of Meldsmead, though she may become a permanent fixture," he said. "I say," he called out to the pair remaining by the window. "Someone else has met our Valerie in the lane and managed to survive." He added to Patrick, "George Kent there met her bonnet to bonnet last weekend. A narrow miss, he had, ha, ha! Miss Valarie," he added, in case anyone had not got the point of his quip.

The crack provoked satisfactory mirth, and on its wave Patrick found himself included in the group. He supplied his own name, and learned that his sponsor was Denis Bradshaw. The third man was Paul Newton.

Patrick had been alerted at the mention of Valerie. From what had been said it seemed that the wild driver he had met might be Miss Amelia Brinton's niece. The other men were continuing to talk about her.

"Is she going to stay on here, George?" Denis asked.

George Kent was a red-faced man with bright blue eyes. He looked cheerful.

"I don't think she's decided yet," he said.

"The lady Jehu you met has just inherited a cottage in the village," Denis explained. "It belonged to her aunt, an odd old woman, very brainy, but nice with it, if you know what I mean. It's down one of the dead-end lanes up there." He gestured in the direction of that part of the village where Patrick had not yet been. "The old girl died about a month ago, rather suddenly. Some sort of accident. Fell down some steps in Greece."

Patrick did not want to let a web of deceit accumulate. "Was that Miss Amelia Brinton?" he asked.

"That's right. Had you heard about it? There was a bit in some of the papers. Turned out the old girl was rather well known in her day. Had a famous father, it seems."

"And the niece?" Patrick prompted.

"She's inherited the lot. Not that there's much except the cottage, I don't suppose, and it's in pretty poor nick. Every wall smothered in books, I should think that's what holds it together, stops the walls falling down. Isn't that right, Paul?"

Paul Newton took his pipe from his mouth.

"There's something in what you say, Denis, as always. But I think the cottage is sounder than you imply. It's been standing a good few years now."

"It's old, is it?" Patrick asked.

"Yes—beamed and thatched," said Denis. "Too quaint for Valerie, I'd guess."

"You hope, you mean," grinned George Kent. "You don't want to risk your neck every time you go down the village street."

"It'll be too quiet here for Valerie," Denis said in a hopeful voice. "Anyway, she'd only use the cottage for weekends. She's got some very high-powered job in London," he told Patrick.

"Can't you commute from here?" Patrick asked.

"Easily," said George. "I do." He finished his beer and glanced at his watch. "Well, I must be off now or Winifred will be after me."

He left them, and through the window Patrick could see him walking briskly down the lane.

"George doesn't spend long in here these days," said Denis. "He's got a pretty new wife, plump, you know, but comely, like the poet said."

Patrick had a feeling he was really quoting the Bible and had got his adjectives confused, but kept silent.

"His second," added Denis. "Can't neglect her."

"Here comes Valerie again," said Paul Newton, who seemed content to remain in the conversational background. "Hope George hears her coming."

They watched the red mini skelter past; it sped on and then swung wildly round to the right.

"She'd a passenger," Paul said.

"Must have been to fetch her from the station," said Denis. "We'll have to train Valerie if she's going to stay on here. Or get her copped. Can't have our lane a death trap. Still, you're usually around, aren't you, handy enough. Paul's a sawbones," he said to Patrick.

Patrick had been wondering what the quiet man did. He was tall and very thin, and had an abstracted expression.

"I'm a pathologist," he said to Patrick. "I don't often get at living bodies. Not that there'd be much of you left alive after a head-on collision with Valerie Brinton." His face took on a more sombre look as he said this.

"Interesting profession," Patrick said, his eyes lighting up. This man must know a great deal about forensic medicine, a subject Patrick found absorbing, to his sister's great disgust: she thought it morbid. "You live here too?" he asked.

"Yes. Up that way, near the church, past George's house. His is just out of sight round the bend."

"Do most people work locally, or are there many commuters?" Patrick asked.

"A good number go to Newbury or Winchester, or even as far as Southampton," Paul said. "George is a stockbroker. He goes up from Newbury, and so do a few more. Denis here has the best of things. He grows vegetables and sells them."

"What does the chap who's bought Abbot's Lodge do?" Denis asked. He spoke quickly, almost cutting into what Paul was saying. Patrick guessed he had been made redundant in middle age and been forced to find a new career; it was a common enough story.

"I didn't know it had been sold," Paul said.

"Oh yes. All signed and sealed, and the new people

move in any day, I believe," said Denis. "They're going to spend a fortune on it, doing it up, so I'm told." He explained to Patrick: "It's down the lane past Mulberry Cottage, where that maniac in the red mini is temporarily installed. Got a terrible reputation. The house, I mean."

So had the unfortunate Valerie, it seemed, though only for her driving.

"Why? Is it haunted?" Patrick asked.

"It was once part of an old abbey," Paul Newton said. "You know how stories grow about these old places. Naturally through the centuries it's seen its share of tragedy. Well, I must go. Nice to have met you, Grant. See you soon, Denis, I expect."

"Certainly," said Denis, and when Paul Newton had gone he said to Patrick, "Clever chap, that, but melancholy. His work, you know. Must be most depressing. And I shouldn't have said that about him mending the victims if Valerie Brinton mowed anyone down in her wild way. His wife was killed in a car smash a couple of years ago."

"Oh dear," said Patrick. "Well, you can't watch every word."

"One forgets, you see," said Denis. "But he doesn't, poor chap. He was at the hospital when they brought her in. She was in an awful mess."

"Has he a family?"

"Rather a nice schoolgirl daughter, and a student son, going to be a doctor. We don't see much of the boy, now, but the girl appears in the school holiday and rides a pony round the place. She's at boarding school. Miss Amelia Brinton, the old girl who died, helped Paul fix it up, in fact. They were great friends, he and Amelia, they used to talk about Egyptian tombs and things. It seems best for the girl after Angela died. Paul's lonely, though. We see quite a bit of him, he plays bridge and so does my wife, and he comes for a meal now and then. You'd think he'd marry again but he seems to be interested only in dead bodies." With this pronouncement, Denis finished his beer. "Well, I must be off now. I live down the lane on the left, Meadow Farm, my place is called. Come in any time if you're back this way."

He called out a farewell to the landlord and was gone. Patrick bought himself another beer and ate his sandwiches, which he had felt unable to tackle during this burst of friendly conversation. The sailing party had produced some charts now, and were engrossed in their plans, though the three women spared him a glance as he sat down in a corner of the bar. But he was prepared too. He took a little book from his pocket and began to read it while he ate. It was a paper-back volume of essays about the tragedies of Shakespeare by one of Patrick's colleagues, whose theories he always tried to demolish when he got the chance.

IV

Later, Patrick drove through the village to the church. He went slowly past a pleasant Queen Anne house, with a well maintained garden separating it from the road. Several houses built of mellow brick were clearly converted from what had once been farm cottages, and there was a small close of neo-Georgian modern houses which would blend in well when their bricks had weathered and their newly laid-out gardens had matured. He wondered where George Kent and his new wife lived, and which was the lonely abode of Paul Newton. In the centre of the village, opposite the post office, was a garage, with a workshop at the side of a row of petrol pumps.

He went into the church, part of which dated from Norman times. In the porch, among notices of service times and posters about charity appeals, was pinned a list of names and dates: the flower-arranging rota shared by women in the parish. He saw the names of Mrs. Kent and Mrs. Bradshaw among others.

Inside the church there were box pews and a fine marble tomb which held the remains of a fifteenth century abbot. A short history in a frame on the wall told the visitor that the church had once been part of the abbey, and remembering the talk in the pub about Abbot's Lodge, Patrick wondered if an abbot's ghost rose from here and stalked across the fields. He went round reading the inscriptions on the walls, and had lifted up a strip of carpet in the chancel to inspect the brass below when a voice behind him spoke.

"Do you want to take a rubbing?" asked the vicar. He was a small man with a round, cheerful face, and he was wearing a cassock.

"No—no. I was merely curious," Patrick said, restoring the carpet to its original position and standing up again. He felt as guilty as a schoolboy caught cribbing.

"It's quite a good one," said the vicar. "We get a lot of people coming in. I never mind if they ask, naturally, but sometimes you find them here, crouched like mantises, just when there's about to be a wedding, or worse, a funeral. It leads to complications. The vicarage is just next door. It's so simple to seek permission first."

"Quite," Patrick agreed, and deemed it wise to introduce himself. As soon as he mentioned his name the vicar looked alert.

"You are the good soul who saw our dear Miss Amelia Brinton to her rest," he said, greatly embarrassing Patrick by this verbal extravagance. "And you wrote such a thoughtful letter. Valerie showed it to me. I should like to see that corner of Athens you described, where she lies now. We were all so shocked by the accident. It was very sad."

"It was horrifying," Patrick said.

"I suggested a memorial service here, but Valerie would not agree. She thought no one would come. I knew the whole village would turn out, but she still refused. We said some special prayers in our ordinary services."

"It was all very proper, in Athens," Patrick said, as he had emphasised in his letter.

"Oh, I'm sure. There is solace in ritual," said the vicar. "Have you come here to see Valerie? She's staying at Mulberry Cottage this weekend."

"No, I just happened to be passing," Patrick said, and explained his presence in Meldsmead. It turned out that the vicar, whose name was Lionel Merry, knew Canon and Mrs. Fosdyke, so they explored this link for some time, until the vicar remembered why he had come into the church, which was to look up something in a register.

"Do call on Valerie if you've time, before you leave the village," he urged Patrick. "She's got Mildred Forrest staying with her. She was a great friend of Amelia's and until this year always went with her to Greece. She has a weak heart and felt she would hold Amelia back if she accompanied her again. A pity. She's grieving for her friend. I think it would comfort her to meet you. Valerie doesn't mean to be unsympathetic but she has little time for the softer side of life, the small deeds that cushion things for others less tough than she is. I suppose it's to be expected. She has an excellent job in industry."

Patrick remembered Valerie's curt little note.

"Was she fond of her aunt?" he asked. "Perhaps she didn't see much of her?"

"She came to stay sometimes. Not often. Amelia respected her very much for her achievements and often talked of her with very great pride. But I sometimes wonder if Valerie has ever had time to grow fond of anyone," was the vicar's sad reply.

"I'll certainly call on Miss Forrest, if you think she would like me to," Patrick said.

"Please do. If you lose your nerve, say I suggested it," said Mr. Merry. "I wish I could invite you to supper at the vicarage, but we have a social in the parish hall tonight and both my wife and I will be out. Another time, perhaps, if you should be this way."

"Thank you," said Patrick.

He walked slowly down the church path back to his car pondering on this exchange. The vicar had painted a not particularly alluring portrait of Valerie Brinton, but surely he did not expect Patrick to shrink from her in fright? She could hardly be more daunting than some of the female dons he knew who were often much cleverer than he was, but who seldom filled him with alarm.

V

Patrick knew which turning to take for Mulberry Cottage because he had earlier seen Valerie Brinton swerving round the corner. He drove slowly down the lane. There were fields on either side, and he had traveled about three hundred yards before he came to a thatched cottage on the left-hand side of the lane. A red mini with a dent in its wing was parked outside. Patrick went past, looking for somewhere to turn, but there were no gateways until he reached the end of the lane where it widened out in front of a large house built of stone. This must be Abbot's Lodge. A high yew hedge concealed most of it from the road, but Patrick could see the leaded windows in the upper rooms, and the tiled roof. There was space for him to swing the Rover round without reversing into the gateway of the house; as he slipped into first gear he heard the deep barking of a large dog somewhere not far away.

Abbot's Lodge certainly was secluded, almost isolated in fact, he thought as he returned the way he had come, and so was Mulberry Cottage. He drew up behind the mini and saw that as well as a dented wing it had a crushed bumper. Then he looked at the cottage. It was very old, probably 17th century, he decided, built of the soft-coloured brick that predominated in the village. The windows were small, the two upper ones peering like eyes out of the fringe of the thatch that framed them. The ridge line of the roof sagged in the middle, and though it was wired, in places the wire had rusted and the birds had made merry with the straw, removing some of it for nests, and in other places burrowing in and building on the spot. A fence, rotted in places, separated the cottage garden from the road, and there was a wicket gate in it that opened on to a flagged path leading up to the front door. There was no garage, and no other gate large enough to let a car in off the road, but there was quite an area of garden around the cottage, filled now with dahlias and michaelmas daisies, and large yellow chrysanthemums.

Patrick got out of the car, opened the little gate, and walked up the path, disturbing a squabble of sparrows who were pecking at the dust between the flagstones. The cottage, except that it was more dilapidated, reminded him of one where Jane had lived for a while when Michael was in America, in a village not so far away from here. Country villages were not always the peaceful places they appeared to be on the surface, and Meldsmead probably had its share of undercurrents like the rest.

A lawn ran away from the cottage at one side, and in the corner, its boughs spreading wide, was a mulberry tree. Patrick was conscious of a movement as he approached the front door, and before he could knock, it was opened. A woman with carroty hair stood before him; she was about forty, of medium height, and slightly built. Her eyes were a brilliant blue, and she was skilfully made-up, wearing lipstick that toned with her well-cut purple trouser suit. Far from being garish, the whole effect was impressive. Patrick found it easy to believe, on her appearance alone, that she was a powerful force in whatever firm she worked for, and he saw the point of the vicar's exhortations.

"Miss Brinton?" he asked, ducking to address her, for the lintel of the door was very low.

"Valerie Brinton. Not Amelia. She's dead," was the uncompromising answer.

"My name is Patrick Grant," he said. "I happened to be passing—"

She interrupted him.

"Oh, Dr. Grant, do come in." Her tone was still brisk, and she did not smile, but she stood back, inviting him to enter. He thought she probably seldom softened more than this.

Bending still further, Patrick entered the cottage. Once inside, he could only just stand upright without touching the ceiling. After the bright, clear day outside it seemed dark at first until his eyes adjusted to the dimmer light within, but the living-room, into which the front door opened, was gloomy. The ceiling was heavily beamed, and the walls were, as he had been told, completely covered with books. Every available space was filled with them. On their knees amongst a pile of volumes on the ground were, he saw, two other women, both staring at him. One got up; she was young and slim, with long dark hair clasped into a slide at the nape of her neck.

"My niece Ellen," said Valerie Brinton. "And this is Miss Forrest, a friend and colleague of my aunt's. Dr. Grant, who was in Athens."

"Oh!" came a little cry from the floor, and Miss Forrest made fluttery movements. Patrick was meanwhile shaking hands with Ellen, who offered him a cool, firm palm. At first glance she bore no resemblance to her aunt except in build.

"Please don't get up, Miss Forrest," Patrick urged the figure on the floor.

"But I must, I've got cramp," said Miss Forrest, hauling herself up by clutching at a chair.

Patrick was a big man, and his presence made the small room seem crowded.

"Mind you don't trip," Ellen warned him. "There are books all over the place."

Patrick's eyes were adjusting to the light, and he took in more details. He saw that Miss Forrest, now upright, was tiny; her neat head was covered with snow-white curls. She came up to him and caught hold of his arm with her two little paws.

"You were so kind to write as you did about poor Amelia," she said, and her voice trembled, with emotion, Patrick thought, and not extreme age.

"We're just sorting out some of my aunt's books," said Valerie briskly. "Milly thought they might be valuable, and anyway I can't possibly keep them. This whole place will have to be done up from top to toe."

"You'll be keeping the cottage, then?" Patrick asked.

"Oh yes. For a time, anyway. I'll do it up and see how things go. I might sell it eventually," Valerie said. "I'd make a bomb."

She would too. She'd enlarge the windows, get all kinds of grants and add heating and so forth. Quite right, really. The place would fall down if it wasn't rescued soon, and olde-worlde charm could pall in cold wet weather.

"You would know about the books," said Ellen.

"What about them?" Patrick turned to her. She had enormous eyes of some dark colour; could it be violet?

"Whether they're valuable."

"I'm not an expert," Patrick said.

"Some of them are first editions," Ellen told him. "They belonged to Amelia's father."

They might, in that case, be of interest to his classical colleagues who were always bemoaning the impossibility of obtaining various out of print works for their own use or as replacements for volumes lost or stolen from the college libarary.

"Mildred is going to spend a week here later, making a list," said Valerie.

"It's so kind of you, dear, to let me. I shall enjoy staying here," said Miss Forrest.

Cataloguing the books would be quite a task, and Patrick wondered if she were physically equal to it. He peered at the nearest shelf and what he saw made him whistle.

"I see you've got a Burmann *Petronius*," he said. "I know someone who'd be very glad to get hold of that."

"Dr. Grant had better have a copy of the list, Milly, when you've done it," Valerie said. "Perhaps you would advise us?" she asked him.

"With pleasure," Patrick said. He could soon enlist more expert advice than his own, and there were some treasures here.

"Milly lives in London and spends her days beetling round museums and art galleries," Ellen said. "She's just the person to do this sort of cataloguing."

"Amelia used to visit me," Miss Forrest said. "And I often used to come here too." She looked wistfully round the room.

"Now Milly, you've done quite enough work for the present," Valerie said. "You take Dr. Grant into the garden while Ellen and I do some clearing up in here and get tea ready." She spoke quite kindly to the old woman. Despite the fizzing image she projected she was not without compassion.

"Oh—very well, Valerie, if you say so," agreed Miss Forrest meekly.

"Do we go this way?" Patrick asked, indicating the front door, and at her nod opened it and stood aside for her. She walked with quick steps down the path and across the lawn. Patrick ducked his head to clear the door as he followed. There was a wooden seat under the mulberry tree and they made their way towards it, Patrick taking one long stride to about three of Miss Forrest's bird-like hops. She was rather out of breath when they arrived; no, she would not have been fit to climb the Acropolis of Athens this summer.

"Earlier in the year mulberries keep landing on one's

head, sitting here," she panted as they sat down. "But it's safe now." Sure enough, the seat and its arms had crimson splodges on them, the dried-out stains of crushed fruit.

Sitting beside her on the bench, Patrick described how he had first seen Miss Amelia Brinton at Delphi, so that he knew her again when they were both looking at the Caryatids. Then he told her about the accident and what followed, stressing the kindness of the Greeks and the British Embassy and minimising the horror of the accident.

"Poor dear Amelia. I am glad she was buried in Greece, she would have liked that. But I shall never see her grave. When you next go to Athens, Dr. Grant, will you put some flowers on it for me?"

Patrick promised to do this.

"She was my friend," said Miss Forrest simply.

Patrick was silent while she extracted a handkerchief from the sleeve of her grey crimplene dress and mopped her eyes with dignified delicacy. Then he said, "She must have been a remarkable woman."

"She was. She had a first-class brain. Some people thought her hard and too inflexible. She could never forgive a girl who let down the high standards she had set," said Miss Forrest. "But one must have ideals. If not, what is there to live for?"

A good question, and one that might with advantage be asked more loudly and more often nowadays, thought Patrick.

After a little prompting, Miss Forrest described some of the holidays she had shared with Miss Amelia.

"She made all the arrangements and took total charge. I just followed where she led, but she made it all come alive for me. I understood the aesthetic side of what we saw, but she was the scholar who made the historical aspect real," she said.

"You will miss her," Patrick said gently.

"Yes. I never thought she would go first, she was

always the strong one," said Miss Forrest. "I'll get used to it. One gets used to anything."

Patrick thought of the cynicism with which the modern world would regard such a friendship between two women and the snide inferences it would prompt. Yet each had probably once hoped to marry; he could easily imagine Miss Forrest during the 1914–18 war on the arm of a subaltern soon to die.

He was going to ask her if she remembered Jane during her last year at Slade House when Valerie and Ellen appeared from the back of the cottage, each with a tray.

There were scones.

"Bought, I'm afraid, from the village shop this morning," said Valerie. "But the jam's home-made. Amelia got it at the church fête, it's Mrs. Merry's strawberry, and famous here."

"And," said Ellen, whose tray bore a yellow earthenware pot with a large bee on the lid, "there is honey still for tea."

Later, she walked with Patrick to the fence that divided the garden from the field beyond.

"I thought no one read Rupert Brooke now," he said to her. "My pupils don't, much."

"Oh," she shrugged. "Perhaps I wanted you to realise I could read and write, in spite of my obvious lack of education."

"You don't seem ill-educated to me," said Patrick, who had given the matter no thought at all. "If you went to Slade House you must have learned a lot."

"I didn't go there. Amelia never forgave my mother for not sending me, even though she'd retired. My father—Valerie's brother—was killed in the war, and my mother married again when I was quite small. I've got two half-sisters and we all went to the local high school. We were very happy there. It's gone comprehensive now."

"You probably had much more opportunity there than you would have at Slade House," said Patrick. She was older than he had thought at first, if she was born during the war.

"Amelia didn't think so. We were a bit short on the classics," Ellen said. "Valerie didn't go to Slade House either. I'm not sure why—probably because she lived abroad. She's a brilliant linguist." She plucked a blade of grass and rubbed it between her fingers. Some heifers in the field had moved closer to the fence and were looking at them both with mild-eyed interest. The beasts' slow movements made the grass rustle. "My stepfather's a dear and I had a very happy childhood. I go home often," Ellen added.

And you've got a giant chip of some sort on your shoulder or you wouldn't be telling me all this, thought Patrick.

"Good," he said, and after a suitable pause to show respect for this unknown man who had made a success of a difficult job, he changed the subject. "Is that the house with a bad reputation?" he asked, pointing across the field to where a wing of Abbot's Lodge was visible above its screening hedge.

"Yes. How did you know about it?"

"I had a sandwich at the pub. Some chap there mentioned it. It's just been sold, hasn't it?"

"Yes. My firm handled it, in fact. I work for an estate agent in London." She named a well-known firm. "We thought we'd have it on our books for ever. People got interested. Then they faded away when they heard the stories."

"What's so awful about it?"

"Oh, the locals say it's an unlucky house. Someone hanged himself there once, and there was a fire, and a couple who lived there during the war split up, and Mrs. Fellowes, the wife of the man who's just sold it, died there."

"In mysterious circumstances?"

"No. But tragically, of leukaemia. She wasn't old."

"Well—these things happen, don't they?" That house must have been standing there for centuries, and witnessed plenty of good things too, like births and golden weddings."

"I suppose so. All the same, it has a funny atmosphere. Sort of hostile. I felt it when I took people round it. Sometimes when the partners are busy I do that kind of job."

"Couldn't it have been just because it was empty?"

"I don't think so. I go over lots of empty houses, I'm used to that deserted feeling. This was different. Almost desolate. I felt rather sorry that we'd sold it, in case it brings bad luck to the new owners."

"You'd better change your job," said Patrick with a grin.

"I don't know why I'm talking to you like this anyway," said Ellen. "Val would laugh the whole thing to bits. But there's something else. The last people who lived there —the Fellowes—looked so like this new couple. They're called Bruce, the new ones. David and Carol. Mrs. Fellowes was pale and fair and thin, and very smart. And he was stockily built, with blue eyes and curly brown hair—very much the same types as the Bruces. And the last couple had a golden retriever, and so have these new people."

Patrick remembered the deep barking he had heard. The Bruces must be down today, inspecting their new property.

"There are lots of brown-haired men with blue eyes about the place," he suggested mildly. "And I expect a good few of them marry slender blondes."

"You think I'm mad," Ellen accused.

"Not at all. I think you're highly imaginative and perfectly delightful, and that you might be happier if you were more ordinary, but it would make you less intriguing," he said in a light voice.

Ellen turned her head away so that he could not see her reaction to this remark, which most modern girls would interpret just as casual banter. She did not answer.

"You can't anticipate the troubles of everyone, and

prevent them, you know," he added, in more serious tones. "Tell me about your aunt. She's not a headmistress, I gather."

At this, Ellen laughed.

"Heavens, no. She'd terrify both the children and their parents. Mind you, Amelia did that too. No, Val's a real tycoon. She did a course in business management, and ran a commercial translation service meanwhile. I told you she's a linguist—she's fluent in four languages, including Russian. Someone spotted her remarkable powers while she was dealing with their foreign correspondence and got her into his organization. She's on the board now—handles their P.R. and most of their overseas negotiations."

"Good for her," said Patrick.

"I'm sure she'd have gone to Amelia's funeral if she could have managed it, but she was in the middle of some high-level deal and couldn't. I think she was in Germany. I might have come, if I'd known, but I was away too. Not that it would have done any good. Amelia wouldn't have cared either way."

"Why not?"

"I told you—she thought me illiterate because I haven't a degree and because I'm not cast in the same mould as the rest of the female Brintons. But I admired her."

"She terrified you," Patrick said.

"Yes, she did," Ellen admitted. "She couldn't tolerate any human weakness." It was a stronger statement of what Miss Forrest had already said. "I shouldn't talk like this about her," Ellen muttered.

"It's all right. No one else can hear you, particularly not the ghost of your great-aunt. And she won't be lurking in the shadows behind you in the future." He paused and looked down at her. "Don't be afraid to be yourself, Ellen," he said gently.

It was something he had said before to undergraduates, who at times imagined themselves to be doing their own thing when in fact they were merely following the herd. Patrick believed most of Polonius's counsel to be wise, but he felt some shock now at giving his advice to a pale, pretty girl with dark hair and the most enormous eyes he had ever seen gazing into his.

"I do hope we meet again, Ellen," he said, and meant it.

VI

"And did you arrange to meet her again?" Jane asked, when Patrick told her all this the next weekend. She and Michael and their small son now lived in a village some twenty miles from Oxford. Michael's firm had moved to one of the new industrial centres springing up in that part of the world; and as they were so near, Patrick often spent Sunday with them.

"We didn't part straight away," said Patrick. "I felt very curious about Abbot's Lodge, and so Ellen offered to take me to see it."

"Splendid," said Jane.

"You're not usually pleased when I'm inquisitive," said Patrick.

"You don't often seem to be in the company of delightful young women," Jane retorted.

"You can't possibly know how I spend my leisure," said Patrick, but he grinned. It was another lovely day; Michael was mowing the lawn and small Andrew was charging around with a miniature wheelbarrow which he loaded with cut grass from his father's big one and then carted importantly off to the compost heap, spilling a good bit of it on the way. "Michael's very tolerant of all that," he added, pointing at his nephew's activities.

"Don't change the subject."

"Well, Ellen walked with me down the lane. Abbot's

Lodge is really rather isolated, as I've said. It's got a huge yew hedge all around it. Lots of clipping needed —it's very overgrown. And it has to be double-fenced on the field side to keep the beasts out, because it's so poisonous. It's quite a big house, and the original part is very old but it's been added to and improved from time to time."

"Did you go in?"

"Oh yes. I hadn't said anything to Ellen about hearing the dog barking, and of course it sprang out upon us, barking loudly but wagging its tail in a genial way. I took all the blame for our trespassing, naturally, but no one seemed to mind. I had the impression Ellen had got to know the Bruces quite well—I suppose she could have, during the house dealings. They seemed pleasant enough—a fairly ordinary sort of chap, rather quiet, and a smart wife. She looked a bit dressed up for a day in the country, in fact."

"No kiddy winks?"

"No. I don't think they've got any. They showed me all round the house, and there was no talk of any of the rooms being for children. I can't think why they want such a big house if there are only two of them."

"Maybe they mean to impress their business friends. Have tycoon house-parties and such," said Jane.

"Maybe. They're going to spend a small fortune on the place, making extra bathrooms and all that. It seemed pretty good to me as it was," said Patrick.

"And did you get a spooky feeling there, like Ellen had said?"

"Yes, I did. At least, that's putting it a bit strongly but I understood what she meant. There was a weird alien sort of atmosphere. I'd believe any tale of haunting told about the house. It'll seem quite different when it's been painted and furnished in the lavish style that's evidently planned, I expect."

"You'll be going down again soon, to see how it's getting on, won't you?" Jane said.

"I might," Patrick agreed. "Valerie Brinton's going to

dispose of her aunt's library, and I'm not going to let a chance like that slip through my fingers. There are books on those shelves that the librarian of Mark's will drool over."

"So that'll give you an excuse to prowl around Abbot's Lodge? What does the man who's bought it do?"

"I don't want to prowl around Abbot's Lodge. My interests are more humbly housed, in Mulberry Cottage," Patrick said. "I expect Ellen will be there quite a bit, helping to clear things up. I don't know what David Bruce does, but it must be pretty lucrative—he had a very nice BMW parked outside the house, and he must have paid plenty for the place, besides what they're going to lash out in alterations. I haven't had time to look him up yet. Maybe Michael will know about him."

"Maybe he will," said Jane. "But it's a great improvement on your past form to find you're more interested in Ellen than in the evil atmosphere of Abbot's Lodge."

"Yes, isn't it?" said Patrick lightly. He did not tell Jane that Ellen, at the sight of David Bruce, had suddenly glowed with a radiance that had made his own spirits plummet, nor did he add that as he and Carol Bruce had followed the other two down some steps that led from the terrace to the overgrown lawn, Carol had slipped on the bottom step and twisted her ankle slightly. She protested that it was nothing, rubbed it briskly and seemed none the worse, but she had gone rather pale.

"You must be careful, darling. That's the second time you've fallen this afternoon," said her husband.

"Is it?" Patrick had asked. He could see something shining on the flat stone of the step where Carol had stumbled.

Carol laughed.

"Yes. I must be very clumsy. I trod on a rotten floorboard in the attic and put my foot right through. No serious damage, though, just torn tights and a scratch."

Ellen was frowning. She made no comment then, but later as she and Patrick returned to Mulberry Cottage she told him that the previous owners of the house had

had all the rotten woodwork renewed and such an accident should not have happened.

"Hm. Is that so? It was odd about that stumble in the garden too," Patrick said.

"Why?"

"There was oil on that step. Fine oil, or grease, like vaseline or olive oil, something that didn't show up darkly. While you and Bruce were giving Carol first aid I had a look at it."

"Someone oiling a mower nearby, or garden shears—" Ellen's voice had trailed off.

"No one's touched that garden with any implement for weeks."

They were silent.

"A poltergeist," Patrick said at last. "Your vicar will have to exorcise it."

"I can't think of a more rational explanation," Ellen said. "Though there must be one. Somebody from the village, trespassing."

"Oil-can in hand? Very unlikely," Patrick said, and added, "Isn't Carol going to be lonely there all day? It's very isolated."

"She doesn't seem to mind. She does some sort of freelance journalism and says she needs peace and quiet to write in. In fact she was much keener on the house than Dav—him. There was another one he liked better, the other side of Newbury. I preferred it too. It had a lovely view. She thought it might be windy. Abbot's Lodge looks out on to all those heavy hedges, but it's very sheltered."

"The hedges could come down," Patrick suggested.

"Yes. That would open it up a bit," Ellen said.

"When do they plan to move?"

"Quite soon. They're going to have most of the alterations done when they're in."

"Those books," Patrick said. "Your great-aunt's library. When Miss Forrest's catalogued them, could I have a list as your aunt suggested? I know some of my colleagues would be interested in them, and in any case

I'd be glad to help dispose of them." The librarian of St. Mark's would never forgive him if he let this chance to acquire some Burmanns pass.

Ellen promised to see that a list was sent to him as soon as it was ready, and Patrick drove away from Meldsmead having arranged to ring her the next time he was in London, in the hope that she would lunch with him. How Jane would approve, he thought, turning from the cul-de-sac that led from the cottage into the main village street. But there wasn't much point in spending time with a girl who appeared to be attracted to another man, albeit a married one, to whom she had just sold a very expensive house. In fact, he was not really sure if it was Ellen herself or the reputation of Abbot's Lodge that he found so fascinating.

PART TWO

Mildred Forrest finished cataloguing Amelia Brinton's books on the day the Bruces moved into Abbot's Lodge. In a way it had been a labour of love, but an arduous one, moving them around, reshelving them, and often being carried back on waves of nostalgia into the past. She felt a sense of achievement, though, now that her task was done. The books were a varied collection: some that had belonged to Amelia's father were very old and she thought might be rare editions; they were bound in leather and the pages were thick and yellowed. There were volumes that Amelia had won as prizes as a girl, and others she had bought through the years or been given by former pupils or by friends. Though possibly only of interest to a limited circle of scholars, the collection must be valuable and Valerie would now have to decide whether to sell it as a whole or part with the books one by one, with the aid of Dr. Grant. Mildred favoured this latter plan; it seemed more personal. Anyway, her part was done now; Ellen would type up the list and a copy would go to Dr. Grant for his advice.

Mulberry Cottage was soon going to be very different. It would look so bare when the books were gone, and Valerie had plans to pull the whole place about. Mildred wondered if she would ever visit it again, and thought it most unlikely. Valerie would intend to ask her, but the weeks would pass with no invitation.

Saddened by these reflections, Mildred made herself some tea, drank it, and ate a bourbon biscuit, her weakness. Then she dozed for a while. She woke to hear the furniture van trundling down the lane from Abbot's Lodge. How happy and excited those two young people must be, moving in to their beautiful new home. She would have liked to ask them round as a gesture of welcome, to sherry: she had half a bottle left, a gift from Ellen who had driven her down in Valerie's car the previous weekend for this second visit since Amelia's death, and was coming to fetch her tomorrow. But the Bruces would be too busy settling in, and anyway it was not her cottage; Valerie might not like her asking people in. The vicar had called, during the week, and stayed to tea, but that was different. However, she could take some flowers round to Abbot's Lodge. No one would object to that, and it would be an appropriate way to wish them well, an action Amelia would have approved.

She went out into the garden and picked a large bunch of the yellow chrysanthemums with which Amelia had annually won prizes at local flower shows; then she set off with some eagerness to Abbot's Lodge.

Dusk was falling and the lights were on in the house. The front drive had been weeded and the grass been cut; someone had trimmed the yew hedge. Miss Forrest had seen builder's vans going back and forth, but a gardener must have been at work too. Already the place looked much less derelict. She approached the house, walking on the new-mown turf beside the driveway, making no sound, and drew level with the windows of what she knew as the dining-room; the drawing-room was on the other side of the house, overlooking the garden. She had been there several times with Amelia to visit poor Mrs. Fellowes in her last illness.

Unnoticed in the dusk as she stood outside, Miss Forrest could see David and Carol Bruce facing each other in the room, and from their attitudes she sensed at once the tension between them. Then she heard, coming through the open window, the sound of David's angry voice.

"I've bought the house you wanted, Carol, and I've given you a blank cheque for doing it up and furnishing it. What more must I do to make you happy?"

Aghast, Miss Forrest saw the rage on his face, and something else: the pain. Then, as she turned to flee before they saw her standing there, all the lights went out.

She stumbled away down the lane, her heart thumping, back to the sanctuary of Mulberry Cottage. Much later she realised that in her agitation she had dropped the bunch of flowers somewhere on the way, but she did not go back to look for them. She did not at once turn the lights on in the cottage but sat gasping in a chair till she got her breath back. When she did try the switch, they worked.

II

Ellen was prompt in sending a typed copy of the book list to Patrick. He glanced down it, whistled to himself, and took it straight round to the librarian of St. Mark's, who was a classical scholar. The library was in fact run by a young man who had trained for the job, but Bernard Wilson was titular chief presiding over all and doing his best to control the committee. Patrick found it politic to keep on good terms with both Bernard and his assistant so as to make sure the proper quota of library funds was spent on behalf of the English department, with an adequate outlay for his own period. Quite often he worked in the library himself, when he wanted to check references; it was on the first floor of the college, a huge room with a high vaulted roof and windows overlooking the college gardens. He found it interesting to observe which of his pupils used the place.

Both Dr. Wilson and his assistant were enthusiastic over several items on the list.

"Look at these Burmanns," Bernard Wilson said. "I'd like to bespeak those, Patrick. Can you arrange it? And there are plenty of other things there, too, that I'd like either for myself or for the library."

"The Burmanns are special, aren't they?" Patrick said.

"Yes, indeed. Published in Holland in the 18th century and never been reprinted—I see there's a set of Ovid here in four volumes, and the *Satyricon* of Petronius—get these for me, I beseech you, Patrick." Bernard Wilson read eagerly on down the list, his eyes alight behind his thick pebble glasses, and his bushy black beard twitching.

"The owner hasn't decided yet whether to break up the collection or deposit it with some bookseller complete," Patrick said.

"It would be more profitable to sell off individual items through us and our colleagues, and then dispose of the rest *in toto*," Bernard said. "We could pay a fair price—Thornton's would advise."

"True enough. I'll do my best," Patrick said.

"These Loebs and Teubners aren't of much value—but it's a chance to replace missing items. I should think the whole library would be worth quite a lot of money," said Bernard.

"I'll tell the owner," Patrick promised. "Leave it to me."

He went happily back to his rooms and had time to write telling Ellen of this reaction and put the letter out in the box for the messenger to mail before his first pupil of the day arrived.

After lunch his telephone rang. It was Jane.

"You're not teaching, are you, Patrick?" she asked at once.

"No. It's all right. What's up? You sound fussed."

"I am. Two things, one good, one bad."

"Let's have the bad one first," said Patrick. It couldn't be Michael or Andrew; she'd be frantic and unable to see good in anything.

"It's Mildred Forrest. The one you met, the little one, Amelia's friend."

"What's happened to her? Is she ill?"

"She's dead, Patrick. It's in the paper today, a tiny paragraph. I noticed it by chance."

"You mean in the obituary column?"

"No. In the home news section tucked away, just a few lines. She had an accident. Patrick, she fell down the stairs of the British Museum."

There was silence on the line.

"Patrick? Did you hear me?" Jane demanded.

"Yes, I heard. I was just rendered speechless," Patrick said.

"It shocked me too," said Jane.

"Which stairs? That entrance flight? Surely that wouldn't kill her?"

"It might, at her age. But it wasn't there, it was inside. I think it must have been that imposing staircase that rises up out of the entrance hall on the left, you know. I suppose she had a heart attack. You said she'd got a weak heart, didn't you?"

"Yes, she had." He remembered how breathless she had been, tripping along beside him in the garden of Mulberry Cottage. "I suppose that must have been what happened. How dreadful, though." Patrick paused. "Jane?"

"Well?"

"It seems to me that too many people have been falling about the place lately."

"I thought you might think that. But it's sheer coincidence. Two elderly ladies, who happened to be friends."

Jane did not know about Carol Bruce's minor tumble.

"She lived somewhere near the Cromwell Road, she told me so," Patrick mused. "Her address might be in the telephone directory."

"I doubt it. Didn't she have just a bed-sitter? Try Ellen, if you want to know more. She'll be sure to have heard what happened, won't she?"

"You mean you actually want me to stick my nose in?" Patrick asked, unable to believe the evidence of his ears.

"Well, she was a nice old thing. I'd like to know what happened. I don't suppose there'll be any more about it in the paper."

"There'll have to be an inquest," Patrick said.

"One of those policemen friends of yours would tell you about that," Jane said. "If Ellen can't, I mean."

"True enough. I'll see what I can discover," Patrick said. "Now, what's the other news, the good bit?"

"I'm pregnant, Patrick. I really am, this time. It's all set," Jane said, and her whole voice changed. "I didn't tell anyone except Michael until it was quite safe. Isn't it wonderful?"

"How marvellous, Jane. I am glad. Take care. Don't get all in a fuss about poor Miss Forrest and upset yourself."

"I won't. In fact I was resting, feet up, you know, all relaxed, when I read it in the paper. Otherwise I'd have missed it."

Jane, longing to provide Andrew with a brother or sister, had had two miscarriages and begun to lose hope.

"So you knew that day when you came to the dentist. I thought you looked rather smug."

"Don't be wise with hindsight. I've been being very careful, no dashing about, but everything's all right now."

"I'm so glad, Jane dear."

"I thought you would be, but you needn't start clucking like a broody hen yourself. You get on with ringing up Ellen. Do you know where to find her?"

"Of course I do. We've been in touch about Miss Brinton's books."

"Oh, have you, indeed? That's nice. Keep it up. And tell me what happens—some of it, I mean. The part about poor Miss Forrest."

"I will. Old ladies do have heart attacks, Jane. She did seem fragile. Probably she just chanced to have hers in rather an unusual spot." Patrick decided to ignore Jane's oblique reference to any dealings he might have with Ellen.

"I wonder what she was doing in the British Museum," Jane said.

"People do go there, dear. I sometimes do myself," said Patrick.

III

Ellen supplied the answer to this question.

"She often went there in cold weather. It's warm, and you can sit comfortably for ages gazing at things and no one disturbs you," she said. "And there's food and a loo and all that, laid on. It saved her heating bills. She lived in a rather grim little bed-sitter. That's why she loved going down to Meldsmead and particularly for as much as a whole week, like she'd just spent there. It was free, there was food in tins already there to eat up, and she felt by listing the books that she was earning her keep."

"Was she as hard up as all that?" Patrick asked.

"Mm. I don't suppose she'd taken out any insurance scheme of her own while she was working, so she had to dip into her savings. And until this year she'd always gone abroad—I expect she had to economise pretty rigidly to find the cash for that."

After Jane's telephone call, Patrick had rung up Ellen and arranged to meet her for dinner the following evening. He had a tutorial and a lecture during the day and could not get up any earlier; in any case, she would have been free only in her lunch hour. Now they were dining in rather a pleasant small restaurant not far from

Covent Garden; the atmosphere was tranquil and the tables were far enough apart to allow some degree of insulation from the conversation of others.

"Poor Milly. Of course it was a heart attack," said Ellen, toying with her smoked trout. "She was flaked out after sorting all those books. I was afraid it might be too much for her. Some of them were pretty heavy tomes, and she dusted them all while she listed them. She should have spent longer doing it."

Patrick had already discovered through his friend Detective-Inspector Colin Smithers that there would be no inquest on Miss Forrest. The autopsy had shown heart failure and multiple fractures. Her little bones must have been as frail as those of a sparrow.

"The awful thing was," Ellen went on, "that I was there."

"What do you mean? In the British Museum with her?"

"In it, but not with her. I was late, and she was dead when I got there. They were carting her out to the ambulance. I didn't realise who it was at first."

"Do you mean you were meeting her?"

"Yes. She'd asked me to. We were going to have lunch together, just a snack, you know, in that subterranean place. I was to meet her in the hall at the foot of those stairs she fell down. I suppose she'd spent the morning upstairs somewhere among the drawings or something."

"Did you often meet her there?"

"No. We'd never done it before. I knew she spent hours in museums and galleries and things because Amelia used to meet her in them. That's how I knew about her being hard up and all that. Amelia used to stay in a private hotel in the Cromwell Road, when she came up to London—Milly hadn't got room for her, but it was always called 'staying with Mildred.' I didn't know her all that well, we'd met a few times of course. She missed Amelia dreadfully. I think she felt her last link with her own generation had gone. I suppose she was still suffering from the shock of it."

"I expect she was." Patrick looked across the table at Ellen. She was looking very pale tonight and there were shadows under her eyes. "Did she have any particular reason for wanting to meet you?"

"She had something to tell me. She said I was right about Abbot's Lodge. That's all she'd say on the phone."

"What do the Bruces think about the house's reputation, or what you said about feeling the atmosphere there to be hostile? You told me that when we were alone in the garden but I suppose you'd mentioned it to her too?"

"Yes, I had. I—the firm, that is—had been trying to find a house for the Bruces for ages, and I was very keen to get something that would be just right for them. I told Valerie and Mildred I wasn't altogether happy about Abbot's Lodge."

"What do the Bruce's think about the house's reputation?" Patrick asked.

"They just laughed about it," Ellen said.

"You told them?"

"I had to. I couldn't let them buy it without knowing about it, I'd got to know them quite well during their search. My boss would probably slay me if he knew I'd tried to put them off it. It's not the way to sell houses."

"Well, the Bruces have been all right so far, haven't they?" Patrick asked.

"I suppose so." Ellen sounded doubtful. "Carol twisted her ankle that afternoon we were there, do you remember? And she'd put her foot through the floorboard earlier. And David said she'd scratched her arm on a rusty nail in the cellar."

David had said so, had he? And when had he told Ellen that?

"Maybe she's just accident-prone," he said lightly. "You've been down again, have you?"

"Yes. I collected Milly the weekend before last, while Val was away in Denmark on some job. She lets me use her car if she's out of the country. Then I met her at Heathrow last weekend and we both went down to

Meldsmead." Ellen took a sip of the excellent claret they were drinking with their pheasant. "We went out to drinks in the village on Saturday evening—people had heard the Bruces had moved in and wanted to be friendly. When we all left, their car—the Bruces', I mean—had a puncture."

"That smooth BMW? What a pity," Patrick said.

"It wasn't David's car. It was Carol's Lancia. It's rather unusual, isn't it, to have complete flats like that? When you're parked? More often tyres go down gently, don't they?"

"Well, yes. But nails and things do lie around," said Patrick. "It doesn't necessarily mean that a ghost from Abbot's Lodge followed the Bruces down the road and slashed the tyre. Where was the party?"

"At the Bradshaws. He's a market gardener who lives down the lane near the church."

Patrick's chatty friend from the pub.

"Was it a good party?"

"Yes, I suppose so, as these things go," said Ellen. "It was prompt of the Bradshaw's to ask them so soon."

"Meldsmead must be a friendly place."

"It is, fairly. Of course, it's so small that any newcomer is an object of curiosity. And Abbot's Lodge has been empty so long that I should think everyone was extra eager to inspect the Bruces."

"What's Mrs. Bradshaw like?" Patrick asked. "I've met him." He had already told Ellen about his visit to the Meldsmead Arms, the day they met.

"Very efficient," said Ellen. "She must be a great blessing to Mrs. Merry—the vicar's wife. She helps with things in the village, bazaars and so on. Denis was in the Army, he took up market gardening when he retired. I suppose Madge got used to running things when they were in the Army, organizing the soldiers' families and so on. I imagine that still goes on."

Patrick felt sure it did.

"What do you do at weekends if you're not at Mulberry Cottage?" he asked her.

"Sometimes I stay in London. Sometimes I go home. I've already told you I get on well with my family," she said.

"You seem to expect me to be surprised," said Patrick mildly. "Even some undergraduates like their parents, oddly enough. In any case, I should think you have few foes."

For some extraordinary reason, as he looked at her, he longed to quote Byron and tell her that she walked in beauty. There was some magic, ethereal quality about her tonight. No female had ever had this effect on him before. He took a stern grip on himself, lest his lunatic emotions be reflected in his face.

"The next time someone's down at Mulberry Cottage I'd like to come over and talk about the books," he said. "Our librarian is very interested in a lot of them."

"You could come almost any time," Ellen said, "I've got a key now, and Valerie says I can go there whenever I like for the moment. She's going to do it up, but it'll take ages to arrange about a grant and all that."

"Would your aunt part with the books individually? She could sell the whole lot to some bookseller, but it might pay her to dispose of them separately, and some of my colleagues would be very anxious to get hold of certain ones."

"You told me in your letter," Ellen reminded him. "I'm sure Valerie would let any of your colleagues take their pick before selling the rest. There hasn't been time to ask her, since you wrote. But I think you can take it she'd agree."

Patrick knew that Bernard would be eager to grab the plums from Miss Brinton's library at the first opportunity. The difficulty would be to avoid having to bring him on the expedition to collect them.

"May I come and pick out a few fairly soon?" he asked. "Is there a chance that you'll be going down there before long?" He did not want to discuss the books with Valerie; he wanted to inspect them with Ellen.

She shrugged.

"I've no plans for next weekend. And the garden should be cleared up before the winter," she said.

Patrick would get a few titles out of Bernard instantly. Then he could take some stalling action. It would be very pleasant to prolong negotiations through the winter weekends; Homer by firelight, with Ellen: what could be more alluring?

She agreed that he might call for her at Mulberry Cottage at noon on the following Sunday and take her to lunch in Andhurst as a preliminary to their bibliographical discussion.

"And your aunt too, of course, if she's there," he said, fervently hoping that Valerie would have other plans.

He drove her back to her flat in Earls Court, where she put a cool hand in his on her doorstep and thanked him for the evening. Before he could take any further action she had opened the door and vanished inside, leaving him gazing at the solid slab of black-painted wood. He got back into the Rover and sat for some minutes staring at the building, imagining her walking up the stairs to her flat, which she had told him was on the top floor. No lights went on, so it must overlook the gardens at the back of the house. She would not look out and see him still below, a faithful sentinel. It was pointless to remain, so he started the car and drove off towards the Westway and the fast road to Oxford. Soon he was cruising smoothly along the M40, back to his celibate quarters at St. Mark's. As he drove, he thought about how he would see Ellen again on Sunday, and he had reached the Beaconsfield by-pass before he started to turn over in his mind the curious fact of Miss Mildred Forrest's wish to talk to Ellen about the reputed jinx on Abbot's Lodge.

PART THREE

Andrew Conway at three years old was an energetic little boy, keenly interested in all that went on around him. Jane often thought he had inherited some of his uncle's curiosity. He still had what was called a rest every afternoon, when he lay on his bed with his teddy bear and a book. Sometimes he did nod off for a short time, but more often he lectured his teddy on the events of the morning, or carried on long conversations with imaginary people. On the Sunday after Miss Forrest's death, when he had been banished in this way, Jane sat on the sofa in the sitting-room with her feet up, looking at the *Sunday Times* crossword, while Michael read the Business Section.

After a time she said: "I wonder how Patrick's getting on."

"Hm? What's he doing? I thought he was coming to lunch," said Michael.

"He cancelled. He's gone down to Hampshire to see that girl," said Jane.

Michael looked at her over the top of his paper.

"You don't mean to tell me that Patrick's seriously interested in someone you've found for him?" he said. "It's your broody condition running away with your imagination."

"I didn't find her for him, he did it himself," Jane said, and frowned. "She may be awful."

"Who is she?"

"Old Amelia Brinton's great-niece. I must have told you. He met her when he called at Amelia's cottage a few weeks ago. He happened to be near there. You know how he does these impulsive things." Michael did. "He took a fancy to her."

Michael knew that Patrick often took fancies to girls, but never strongly enough to want them permanently around.

"Don't count on it lasting," he advised. "Patrick's pretty set in his ways. He's probably happiest flitting from flower to flower. What's this one's particular charm?"

"He hasn't told me. I just know she's somehow different from the others in the past. And she's muddled up with all these old ladies who keep falling down stairs," said Jane. "You know, Amelia in Athens, and now Miss Forrest in the British Museum."

"They chose some pretty illustrious stairs on which to expire," said Michael.

"Like being run over by a Rolls, you mean? I know. But there's a third one. Patrick only told me about her the other day, when he cried off for this weekend. It's a woman in Meldsmead who fell down some steps in the garden and twisted her ankle."

"She didn't die?"

"No. And she isn't old."

"Anyone can have a domestic accident," said Michael.

"You're starting to talk like Patrick," Jane complained.

"What's wrong with that? I know you love him dearly. In fact I've always thought there was something Grecian, or do I mean Egyptian, like the Pharaohs, in the brotherly love between you," said Michael, grinning at her.

"I won't be provoked," Jane said, looking prim.

"You'll hate it if he marries. Some other woman muscling in when you've him and me, ready to dance to your tune," Michael went on. "And Andrew will join your band of adorers—he has, in fact, though his powers are limited still."

"If Patrick could only be half as happy as we are, I'd rejoice," Jane said, very seriously. "But I'm afraid for him."

"He's probably only buttering this girl up because he's intrigued by something in the set-up," said Michael. "The old ladies and their tumbles, perhaps."

"There's something odd about one of the houses in Meldsmead. The one where the other woman fell and twisted her ankle. It's ill-fated in some way," Jane said.

"Well, there you are, then. He wants some problem to chew over, so he's found one. This girl's just an excuse. Don't worry about it. He's got a genius for getting mixed up with odd types, I agree, but he won't marry one."

"He's been around so often when people are up to no good, I sometimes wonder if he acts as a sort of catalyst. By just being there, perhaps he sets off the chain of murky events."

"Darling, don't be crazy. It's just chance. He's happened to be present when people have died in mysterious circumstances once or twice, and being Patrick, he's seen more of what's gone on under the surface than other people."

"There's something bothering him about Miss Forrest," Jane said. "Poor old Amelia's death really was a most unlucky accident—some rough youth rushed up those steps leading up to the Acropolis and jostled against her when she was standing above a sheer drop, and she fell. Someone younger wouldn't have, or if they did, would have bounced."

"And Miss Forrest got dizzy. Bad heart, wasn't it? Maybe she shouldn't have walked up the stairs."

"I'm surprised she did. There are lifts," said Jane.

"Perhaps she went up by lift and was walking down," Michael suggested. "That would seem reasonable. There must have been witnesses."

"Oddly enough, there were very few people about at

the time, Patrick said. Evidently no one else was on the stairs. She pitched down on her head."

"Well, she wasn't pushed if no one else was around," said Michael. "You usually ridicule Patrick when he gets these fanciful notions."

"I know. But he's been right before, so I'm beginning to take him more seriously," Jane said. "When he suspects foul play, I mean, like they say in the papers."

"Well, he doesn't suspect it this time. He's just using it as an excuse to get together with this dolly-bird, and good for him," Michael chuckled.

"That's the direct opposite of what you said a moment ago," Jane declared triumphantly. "You said she was an excuse to get a foot in that house with the bad reputation."

"Well, it doesn't much matter which way round it is, really, does it?" Michael asked. "If he's having an affair, that's fine, and his business. If he's doing a bit of sleuthing, he probably won't do any harm even if he does no good."

"Miss Forrest had asked that girl to meet her at the British Museum," Jane said. "She wanted to talk to her."

"What an odd place to choose for a rendezvous," said Michael.

"Oh, I don't know. There are plenty of seats about, and it's quiet. You can talk. Patrick said Miss Forrest often went there."

"Well, maybe he'll bring the girl to see us. When he does that, you'll know he really is interested," Michael said. "Then you can start planning Andrew's page's outfit."

11

Patrick, in his eagerness to see Ellen again, had reached the turning to Meldsmead at half-past eleven. She wouldn't be up yet, or she'd be washing her hair, or whatever girls did on Sunday mornings, he thought, feeling strangely unsure of himself. He shouldn't arrive early. He drove on past the turning for half a mile, until he came to a lay-by at the side of the main road, pulled in, and got out of the car. There was a gate into the field beside where he had parked, padlocked. He climbed over it and walked across the grass, which was quite dry as there had not been much rain recently. When he had gone a little way into the field, he could see the village of Meldsmead before him, spread out below. The church tower stood out against the pale autumn sky; the trees had shed most of their leaves, exposing buildings that would not be visible from this point in summer. The cluster of houses that made up the village huddled together in a wide valley; a wood rose up a little hill in the distance beyond, and a stream ran through the fields below where he was standing. He could see Abbot's Lodge, it stood apart, to the right of the village, its mellow tiled roof dull red in the thin sunlight. A grey blob some distance from it must be the thatch of Mulberry Cottage. His binoculars were in the car, and as there were still twenty minutes to occupy before it was time to call for Ellen, he went back for them.

In the field once again, he trained the glasses on Abbot's Lodge. There was a dark hedge round the house. No smoke spiralled from the chimneys, so it must have a modern central heating system installed. As he watched, he saw a figure emerge, apparently through the hedge, and start walking over the fields to where a row of willows, leafless now but pollarded, though not for some years, indicated the course of the stream. It was a man. It must be David Bruce. He walked across the meadow, and at his heels followed the golden retriever whom Patrick had seen before. Then he saw another figure approaching from the opposite direction; slight, in slacks and a dark jacket, with her hair tied at the nape of her neck, Patrick would have recognised Ellen without the binoculars. She was coming from the far side of the stream, and they met on a bridge that crossed it. With a sense that he was spying, Patrick lowered the glasses and turned away; all his elation left him. He put the glasses back in the case and locked them in the boot of the car. Then he got a chamois which he kept in the compartment of the dash, pressed the screenwashers, and busily wiped the windscreen till it shone. After that he walked up the road for two hundred yards in the direction of Winchester, turned and walked back again, and looked at his watch. It was four minutes to twelve. He got into the car, started the engine, and drove to Meldsmead.

When he reached Mulberry Cottage and stopped at the wicket gate in the fence Ellen immediately appeared. Her hair was drawn back into a big slide at the back of her head and she wore a blackberry-coloured trouser suit. She seemed pleased to see him.

"Hullo. You're very punctual," she said. "It's a beautiful day."

"Gorgeous," Patrick agreed, with his eyes fixed on her.

"I mowed the lawn this morning. That should fix it for the winter, don't you think?" she asked. She seemed animated and happy, more than he had ever seen her before. Perhaps she had just bidden farewell to David, for good, Patrick thought, on a fanciful tide of rising hope. His own spirits revived. He admired her handiwork in the garden. The flowerbeds had been forked over and the grass edges trimmed. A few roses still bloomed.

"Do you like gardening?" he asked her.

"It's peaceful," she said. "I don't know much about it, but it's nice to see a reward for your labours."

Andhurst was ten miles away. Patrick had already booked a table at an excellent pub which he knew of in the little town. He successfully expelled from his mind all dark thoughts about Ellen's earlier meeting with David Bruce; it was wholly innocent and accidental, he decided.

When they got back to Mulberry Cottage, Ellen made coffee and they settled down to the books. Patrick had a list of twenty titles which Bernard Wilson wanted, including the Burmanns. More would be wanted by the college and by other classicists once Bernard had picked the best for himself, and they had decided the fairest method of pricing them was to enlist the help of a specialist antiquarian bookseller.

"But your aunt might like to get her own expert," Patrick said.

"I'm quite certain she trusts you and the librarian of St. Mark's not to do her down," said Ellen demurely.

They packed the books into two large cardboard boxes which Bernard had provided. Patrick looked round the shelves.

"It's a marvellous sight, isn't it? A room full of books," he said.

"Yes, if one could only read them," said Ellen ruefully. She pulled one at random from the shelves and looked inside, made a face and put it back. "I suppose you can read them all," she said.

"I can't. With enormous difficulty I might make out the Latin, but not the Greek," he said.

"What's your subject, then? I somehow thought it must be classics, because you were in Athens I suppose," she said.

She knew nothing about him. Only his name. His spirits plunged once more. They had talked about

Rupert Brooke, and she hadn't made the mental connection when he talked about his pupils. But why should she, after all, he thought dismally.

"English," he said. "I'm particularly interested in Shakespeare." As she had done, he now plucked a book from the shelves without looking at it and turned the pages over. He wanted to avoid looking at her for a moment.

"He knew it all, didn't he," said Ellen. "About people I mean. How they behave. Power, and all that, and jealousy. Things haven't really changed a great deal."

"No, they haven't," Patrick said. He reached to put the book back, since now they were to talk. It was a volume of Cicero's *Orations*, the blue-bound Oxford edition, Volume IV. "Hullo, that's odd," he said, pausing with his hand on the space from which he had taken the book.

"What is?"

"I thought that set was complete. Cicero's *Orations* in six volumes. Volume five doesn't seem to be here."

"Is it on Milly's list? Let me look."

Ellen took the list from the floor in front of him. They were both sitting on the carpet with their empty coffee cups beside them. As she moved, a strand of her hair brushed against his face.

"'Cicero: Orations, six volumes,'" Ellen read. "And see, she's noted that the *Letters* are three volumes in four parts, volume two in two parts. She's been very thorough."

"She'd have noticed if volume five was missing?"

"I'm sure she would have. Maybe it's slipped down the back somewhere." Ellen pulled out several of the books and looked about, but there was no sign of it. "How very strange," she said.

"It'll turn up, I expect," Patrick said. "Maybe it got replaced wrongly. I'll make a little note so that we find it later."

He wrote in the margin of the list.

"This looks a rather ordinary, unglamourous sort of

edition, compared with most of Amelia's books," Ellen said, surveying them.

"It's a good working set. I'd have expected your great-aunt to have the Teubners—she did, here they are. But they're old and much used. Probably she lent these to pupils, these newer ones," he said. "She wouldn't risk her more precious ones."

"You're right I expect," Ellen said.

"I'm sure we'll want the Teubners," Patrick said. "What I'm taking now is only a first bite."

"You'll want to come down again, when you've had more time to consult with your friends," Ellen said.

"If I may," said Patrick, and Jane would have been amazed at his diffident air.

"That's all right," said Ellen in a matter-of-fact voice. "You can let me know when you want to come. I can manage almost any weekend."

She sat there with Mildred's list in her hand and Patrick looked at her.

"Ellen?"

"Well?"

"We have Ladies' nights at Mark's now and then, when we invite ladies to dinner. Will you come one day? I'll fetch you—or meet you in Oxford if you'd come for the weekend. I—there's a spare room in my set but it would be more suitable if I arranged for you to stay at the Randolph." He was floundering desperately, but he must make her understand. He hoped she'd realise he meant to pay. He gazed at her earnestly through his heavy-rimmed spectacles. A lock of fine, dark hair fell forward over his forehead.

"When are you inviting me for?" Ellen asked primly.

He could scarcely believe his ear. She would come! He plunged.

"Saturday week," he said. "Please come."

"You really want me to?" She was looking at him doubtfully.

"I do," he said firmly. He had very seldom invited a

woman to dine at Mark's who was not a don, a pupil, or a relative.

"The talk will be miles above my head."

"It won't. Why should you think that? Dons are just people."

"All right. Thank you. I accept," said Ellen.

"Oh, that's wonderful," said Patrick, beaming.

"You'll stay for tea?" said Ellen, suddenly becoming formal. "There are only biscuits. Shall we go for a walk first?"

She got up and moved away from him, towards the window.

"A walk would be lovely," said Patrick, like a polite little boy. "Where shall we go? Across the fields?"

"If you like. There's a stream in the field beyond the garden and it's a bit wet in spots. I've got boots, but what about you?" She looked at his feet in their dark leather shoes.

"I've got some in the car. I keep them there for when I go to see my sister," said Patrick. "I'll get them."

He fetched them from the Rover and changed into them outside the door of the cottage, putting his shoes inside. Ellen joined him. She had tucked the ends of her tweed slacks into a pair of wellingtons. Patrick could see traces of damp mud clinging to them. Of course she had dug the garden, but that must have been the day before; she would not have worn wellingtons to mow the lawn. This mud had come from the field, but she made no reference to having been that way earlier in the day as they set out across the meadow towards the stream.

The few heifers grazing in the field took no notice of them as they passed, busy cropping the last nourishment from the grass before the winter. When they reached the stream they followed its course towards the bridge, which Patrick could not make out quite clearly. It was a rustic affair, a few planks with a handrail, and willows guarded it on either side.

"It's dry enough now, but the stream gets quite deep

in winter, and these meadows sometimes flood," Ellen told him. "You find kingcups in the spring."

They paused for a few moments on the bridge and watched some leaves and twigs slowly drifting down. Two hundred yards away, the dark yew hedge hid Abbot's Lodge from prying eyes.

"How are the Bruces settling in?" Patrick asked, as they resumed their walk on the further side of the stream.

"Well enough, I think," Ellen said lightly. "They've scarcely begun on the alterations. A bit of painting's been done. But Carol means to have a completely new kitchen."

"What do you think Miss Forrest wanted to tell you that day, at the B.M.?" Patrick asked.

"I can't imagine. Maybe she'd heard some fable about the house—more definite than what we'd already said, like the ghost of a monk or something. She may have heard people in the village chatting. It was probably nothing, really. Anyway, we'll never know now."

"No, I suppose we won't," Patrick agreed. They walked on, following the course of the stream which looped round close to the boundary of Abbot's Lodge; they were near enough to see the stout fencing that kept the grazing cattle away from the menace of the yew hedge. Just as they were about to turn back, Patrick caught sight of something in the water.

"Hullo, what's that?" he muttered, and strode forward to the edge of the little stream. He clambered down towards the water, the bank crumbling a little under his weight, and pulled aside some reeds that grew at the edge. Ellen, close behind him, saw it almost as soon as he did.

"Oh no!" she cried. "Oh, it's Rufus."

The Bruces' golden retriever lay on his side underneath the water, quite sodden, and quite dead.

III

Patrick lifted the dog out and laid him on the bank. Water streamed from his thick coat which clung to his body. He was surprisingly heavy, and he was very cold. Bits of weed and vegetation were tangled in his hair, and his tail drooped, its fine featheriness totally obliterated.

"He's been dead for some time," Patrick said. But he had been alive at twenty minutes to twelve that morning.

"How could it have happened?" Ellen's face was white with shock and her eyes huge. "Dog's can swim. Anyway, the water's not deep, he could stand in it. He hasn't been shot or anything, has he? There might have been boys out with air guns."

Patrick carefully turned the body over. There seemed to be no mark anywhere.

"We'd better get Bruce," he said. "We'll need a sack or something to carry him. I suppose he's at home? Are you all right, Ellen?"

She nodded.

"Just horrified," she said. "We can get through the hedge over there and go across the garden."

They walked together, without talking, along the path that he had earlier seen David Bruce take. Here the grass was worn into definite track; either this route was often taken from the house, or it was the way the cattle used. There was a stile in the wooden fence which separated the yew hedge from the field; they climbed it, and opened a wrought-iron gate that led into the garden of Abbot's Lodge.

"We'd better go round and ring the front door bell, I suppose," said Ellen, a little uncertainly.

"Perhaps they'll see us coming," Patrick said.

Someone had clearly been busy in the garden since he was last there; the grass had been cut, and several of the beds were ready for planting, though others were still over-grown. They walked up the stone steps where Carol had twisted her ankle and round the side of the house. David Bruce was there in the yard, washing his car. He had the hose on, and did not hear them coming. They went round to the far side of the car and he started with surprise when he saw them suddenly appear. He could tell at once from their expressions that something was wrong, and immediately laid down the hosepipe and turned off the tap.

"What's up, Ellen? You look as if you've seen a ghost," he said.

"It's your dog," Patrick said bluntly. "I'm afraid there's been some sort of accident. We found him in the stream. He seems to have been drowned."

"Drowned? Rufus? But how could he—it's impossible —" David gaped at them.

"I know. It seems like that, but it's true. We were walking by the stream and we found him," Ellen said. "Patrick got him out, but he's very wet indeed and it needs two people to carry him."

"He was Carol's dog," David said.

Patrick saw Ellen's look of surprise at this information, but she said nothing.

"We'd better tell her then," he suggested. He had already noticed that both the garage doors were open and there was no sigh of the second car; Ellen had said Carol had a Lancia.

"She's out," David said. "She's visiting some house she wants to write about."

"Perhaps it's just as well, since the dog is a rather pathetic sight," said Patrick. "We can deal with it before she comes back. Have you got a sack or a tarpaulin or something?"

"What? Oh, yes. There'll be something in the cellar," David said.

He went off towards the house and down a flight of steps outside the back door.

"We'll cope with this. Don't you come, Ellen," said Patrick.

"I don't want to stay here by myself," said Ellen. "Carol might come back and I'd have to explain."

"Funk sticks, eh?" said Patrick, in a gentle voice.

She nodded. He longed to touch her, to make some sort of physical contact, but his hands were damp from touching the dead, wet dog.

"Why not go back to the cottage, then? I'll come along as soon as we've finished here."

"Perhaps that would be best," she said. She looked sheepish. "Sorry to be feeble. After all, it's just a dog, not a person."

"Well, he's a big dog. That somehow makes it more shocking," Patrick said. And more difficult to account for, he thought. "Make that tea we were going to have."

"All right. I'll have another look for the Cicero too."

"You do that," Patrick said. "We shouldn't be too long. I'll have to help Bruce see to things."

She knew he meant to bury the dog.

"I understand. I'll be off, then."

She left, and David Bruce emerged from the cellar carrying a sack as she passed the head of the stairs. Patrick saw him look at her, but she went unsmiling past, without a word.

"Ellen's a bit shaken, so she's gone home," said Patrick shortly. "The poor brute does look very pathetic. Where shall we bury him?"

"Oh, I don't know," said David. "I'll think of somewhere while we fetch him." Patrick forbore to point out that he owned at least four acres of land, much of it wild orchard. A suitable grave should not be difficult to find.

"That sack won't be big enough," he said. "Have you a knife or something? If we slit it, we could sling the dog in it and carry it between us. I could have brought him back myself but I thought it would upset Ellen."

"You were quite right. Anyway I'd like to see where it

happened. I can't understand it," David said. "He was my wife's dog, but he spent most of his time with me. I was fond of him." And indeed he looked almost as shaken as Ellen had.

He went into the house and returned with a large kitchen knife which he used to slit the sack so that it made a sheet. Then he went back into the house with the knife. A tidy man, Patrick thought.

They walked together to the stream.

"Was he an old dog? He doesn't look it," Patrick asked.

"No, he was only five," David said. "I got him as a puppy."

Heart failure was unlikely, then, as the cause of death.

"Wasn't it difficult, having him in London? Isn't that where you lived?" Ellen had told Patrick that the Bruces had lived in London. "A big dog like that must need a lot of exercise."

"We lived in Putney. I used to take him on the heath. And Carol gets about a good bit in her work. She took him with her sometimes. But it was better for him here, he loved it, running in the fields."

They could see the pale blob of the dog's body on the bank of the stream long before they reached it.

"My God! You poor old fellow," said David, bending over it. As Patrick had done, he turned it, lifting the limbs, searching for any mark.

"Boys? Hooligans?" Patrick asked, thinking of adolescents who cut tails off cats.

"Very unlikely. Meldsmead isn't like that," David said.

"He couldn't have just tumbled in," said Patrick. "Will you get the vet?"

"I'd like to know what happened, but I think it would be very upsetting," David said. Patrick wanted to know too, but even if there was an autopsy it would be difficult for him to learn the results. Ellen might tell him, perhaps.

They spread the sack on the ground and lifted the dog

on to it. A smell of wet hair rose from him. They wrapped the sack around him and lifted it by the ends, but the bundle was dripping by the time they reached the garden of Abbot's Lodge again.

"I wonder if we should bury him before Carol gets back?" David said. "She might want to see him."

"Well, you saw how upset Ellen was, and he isn't her dog," Patrick said. "Wouldn't it be better to get him out of sight, if you're not going to call in the vet?"

"I suppose you're right," said David. "Very well. We'll bury him in the rough grass over there." He pointed to an area under some trees where probably, in the spring, daffodils bloomed. Or if they don't they ought to, Patrick thought.

"You could put a rose tree over him, one of those big spreading ones, what are they called, they turn into a great bush, my sister has one," he said, getting carried away by what Jane would have called his marshmallow streak. "Nevada, that's the name. It's lovely and grows huge."

"I'll remember it," David said austerely. He obviously thought the idea a poor one.

They chose a spot.

"I'll get a couple of spades. You wait here," David said. He seemed to assume Patrick would see the operation through. He would, of course.

It was a morbid task. They dumped the dog on the ground and while David went off to the tool shed, which was part of the stable block, Patrick sauntered along looking at the various trees and shrubs in that part of the garden. He was no horticulturist, but since Jane's marriage he had often lent her a helping hand in the garden, first in the rented cottage she had lived in at Winterswick, and later when Michael and she had bought their present house. He could recognise most ordinary trees and common flowers, and the Fellow's garden at St. Mark's was famous for its herbaceous border. He saw some lilacs, and what he thought must be a forsythia, and another, tall tree with a slender stem and slim, spreading branches. Under it a few seed pods lay on the ground. He picked three or four up and put them in his pocket.

David returned with the spades.

They marked the space to be dug and took out a deep trench, first lifting off the turf neatly for easier replacement.

"Six feet it has to be in the churchyards, I believe," said Patrick, labouring on. They settled for about four in this case, laid the dog in the narrow slit, and shovelled back the rich soil. There was quite a hump when they had replaced the turf on the top.

"We could have carted some of the soil away and then it wouldn't have shown," David said.

"I imagine it will soon drop," Patrick said.

"Maybe."

The thought ran through Patrick's mind that perhaps David meant not to tell Carol what had happened, but to let her assume the dog had disappeared. He banished the notion instantly; Carol would tell the police the dog was missing. Why had such an idea even crossed his mind?

"Well, that job's done, then," he said, and handed his spade to David. "I'm sorry about it. I don't suppose you'll ever know what really happened. Now, if you'll excuse me, I'll get back to Ellen."

He enjoyed saying this, but the other man's face gave nothing away.

"Thanks for your help," he said.

Patrick gave a slight wave, and hurried off across the garden, leaving David to follow with the spades. He walked quickly down the lane and let himself through the gate of Mulberry Cottage. As he walked up the path to the door he heard the sound of a car approaching. Carol Bruce had come home.

PART FOUR

The following Wednesday two of Patrick's pupils asked if they might switch their tutorials to different days, and thus suddenly free, he went up to London. He drove straight to Bloomsbury and found a parking meter near the British Museum. A fine drizzle was falling as he approached the building through the main gate. There were a few coaches parked in the forecourt, and some clusters of schoolchildren were being herded towards the entrance. Patrick decided that this particular temple lacked external magic; Pentelic marble, antiquity, and clear blue skies were necessary for spell-casting. He went inside and walked to the foot of the staircase which led out of the main hall. Here poor Miss Forrest had tumbled to her doom, but no trace of this recent tragedy seemed to lurk in the atmosphere; the usual air of controlled bustle prevailed. It was still early in the day, and at this time of the year there were few tourists about. Patrick wanted to visit the lonely caryatid, but first he walked slowly up the stairs. Halfway up there was a small landing; then the steps continued with another flight, and where they divided to branch right and left there was a wider landing and some seats covered in black leather. He sat there for a while, watching what went on below and meditating. People came and went down in the hall; others climbed up or descended the stairs, sometimes in groups and sometimes singly. After a few minutes he continued upwards himself to the central saloon, where he was in Roman Britain. This was a part of the museum he did not know well, though occasionally he went to the King's Library, and passed through the Grenville Library. He used the Reading Room at intervals, but rarely. Before his recent visit to Greece he had spent hours studying the Parthenon frieze and the marbles from the pediment, and he knew his way round the ground floor well, but this upper floor was less familiar.

He went downstairs again to the busy publications department and bought a guide map; then he returned to the half landing on the staircase where he sat down and studied it. After that he set out to explore a route. He found that by going through the Greek and Roman life room, on past innumerable Greek and Roman vases, turning right through the upper Egyptian galleries as if aiming for the Prints and Drawings gallery, he came eventually to the north stairs, which were richly carpeted in bilious green. Down he went, and was at once on known ground outside the north library. In a very short time he had gone through the King's Library and the Grenville Library and was back again at the foot of the main staircase down which Miss Forrest had fallen.

If someone had known she would be on the front staircase that morning, followed her, and pushed her, he —or she—could have followed the route he had just taken and arrived back in the hall in time to observe the resulting confusion. Or, if they had not wanted to witness the scene, they could have left the museum by the north entrance and disappeared into Montague Place.

But who could have wanted to do such a thing? And who would have known that Miss Forrest would be in the British Museum that day?

Ellen had known, and Ellen had been present.

She must, of course, have arrived, as she had said, a

little late for their appointment, to find the accident had happened. But she could have told someone else about her arrangement to meet Miss Forrest: David Bruce, for instance, or Valerie.

But neither of them could have had the slightest wish to kill harmless Miss Forrest. No, it was just coincidence that the two old ladies, friends in life, had met their deaths in similar ways.

He wandered away, through the throng in the publications department and into the quiet haven of the Nereid Room. There he stood brooding for a long time in front of the solitary caryatid.

After a while he went into the Duveen Gallery and took a look at the model of the Acropolis, but it did not depict the monuments as they were today and the steps leading up to the Propylaea were not restored in their present form. He took a quick tour round the huge room and was about to leave through the glass doors when he saw, seated outside, confronting the enchanting little temple-like building of the Harpy Tomb, David Bruce and Ellen Brinton. They sat close together, earnestly talking, totally oblivious to their surroundings. Nearby stood an attendant carefully ignoring them. Many assignations must be made in these chaste surroundings, Patrick supposed grimly.

He rushed back again into the sanctuary of the Duveen Gallery and stood scowling at a metope showing a particularly fierce centaur. The absorption between David and Ellen had been intense and unmistakeable. After a while he approached the doorway again and peered through. They had gone.

Patrick had intended to ring Ellen at her office and invite her out to lunch. Instead he went straight back to his car, drove to Oxford very fast, and spent over an hour on the river in a skiff, furiously rowing.

Late that night he did telephone Ellen at her flat. He held on while the number rang thirty times without an answer; then he gave up.

II

The next evening Patrick drove over to Meldsmead again. He arrived at about half-past six and went straight to the pub, this time parking in the yard at the rear, for his white Rover was distinctive; it was very unlikely that Ellen would be in the village in the middle of the week, but if by any chance she had come down, he did not want her to see his car. He found Denis Bradshaw alone in the saloon bar, talking to the publican, Fred Brown. They remembered him, and Denis insisted on buying his pint.

"It's still too early for any of our regulars, isn't it, Fred? Thought it must be a foreigner when you opened the door," Denis said, with a grin.

"Do you come in every evening, then?" Patrick asked.

"I do when my wife's out, if I'm not too busy to stop work," Denis said. "Madge is off somewhere playing bridge. She won't be home yet. There are others who come in nightly, though, luckily for Fred."

"Oh?"

"Newton does, on his way back from the hospital. Needs bucking up, I should think, after messing about with dead bodies all day, and I expect the house is a bit bleak when the kids are away. He doesn't come in when they're at home. And the new chap, Bruce, he comes in most days, doesn't he, Fred?"

"That's right. Gets in about seven. He won't be in tonight, though. He said yesterday he'd be staying up in London. He does that once or twice a week, seemingly."

"His wife is often away, too," Denis said. "She's some sort of writer—goes off photographing people and houses and writing about them for those magazines women read at the hairdresser's. Is she better, Fred?"

"I don't know. I haven't seen her car go by today," said Fred. He added to Patrick: "She's got one of those Lancias. Some job."

"And very nice too, but pricey," said Denis.

"Has she been ill? Mrs. Bruce?" Patrick asked.

"Mm, yes. Funny business, that." Denis shook his head. "She's so like Hesther Fellowes to look at. Don't you think so, Fred?"

"I hadn't thought about it, but now you mention it, I suppose she is," said the other man. "Tall, and pale, and thin, but dressier, if you get my meaning."

"Her illness?" prompted Patrick.

"She's not been herself since the dog died—oh, you wouldn't know about that." Denis rushed eagerly into the story, giving Patrick no chance to confess that he did. "The Bruces had a golden retriever—lovely dog, he was, belonged to the wife in fact. He got drowned last weekend. Young Ellen Brinton was staying here at Mulberry Cottage with some boy-friend of hers and the fellow found him in the stream."

Patrick almost choked into his beer. If the identity of Ellen's companion were to be disclosed he would have landed himself in a morass of deception.

"How could a dog drown?" he asked, sinking even deeper.

"You may well ask. He may have eaten something that disagreed with him and gone to the stream looking for water. Might have got hold of some of the dehydrating rat-poison stuff."

His glass was empty and Patrick signed for Fred to refill it.

"Hesther Fellowes had a dog too, and it was a golden retriever," said Denis. Over their second pints he told Patrick how this dog had been found, after her death howling inconsolably in the graveyard, and had eventually been put down.

"The dog would have had to have got hold of a deal of that poison to be affected," Fred said.

"And Mrs. Bruce?" Patiently Patrick returned to her.

"Oh, the vicar's wife discovered she wasn't well," Denis said. "You know, in a village this size we all know each other's business, eh, Fred? Anything unusual gets noticed. Mrs. Merry was in the Post Office yesterday and she saw the doctor's car go down the lane towards Abbot's Lodge, so off she trotted to find out what was wrong. Some sort of gastric upset, I believe."

As Patrick was absorbing this information the door of the bar opened and in came Paul Newton, followed by two of the other men who had been discussing yachting when Patrick was in the Meldsmead Arms before. If everyone knew each other's business as definitely as Denis Bradshaw seemed to think, his own presence in the village would soon be revealed.

"Ah, Paul. Cut up any interesting bodies lately?" Denis asked heartily.

The tall, pale pathologist sighed.

"Denis, I keep trying to explain to you that I don't deal with bodies. Other pathologists do, but I test blood and I look for bugs. It's a wide subject, you know."

"And a gloomy one," said Denis. "Well, I must go. Madge told me to do something about turning on the oven. We've got an automatic switch but it's gone wrong."

He finished his drink and went off into the night. Paul Newton remembered meeting Patrick; they talked generalities for a while and discovered, as so often happens, a link, for Newton had a nephew who had been up at Mark's. Luckily Patrick remembered the boy from his days as dean; luckily too Patrick could recall only points in his favour. They talked about this for a while and then Patrick asked the other man what he thought about the reputation of Abbot's Lodge. He remembered that at their earlier meeting Paul had said stories always circulated about old houses.

"One does get a run of bad luck—or of good, come to

that, sometimes," said the doctor. "It's convenient if you can blame it on your environment, I suppose, and not yourself or just the luck of the draw. Certainly the Bruces seem to have had more than their share of minor misfortunes since they moved in. You heard about the dog?"

"Yes." Patrick wondered if the other would volunteer a theory.

"Odd, that. I'd like to have known the cause. But Bruce buried the dog without investigation. Less distressing for his wife, no doubt."

"She's ill now, I hear," said Patrick.

"So I believe."

"Have you met them?"

"Yes. Denis and Madge had a party to introduce them round. He seems a decent enough chap, rather quiet. Does something in the city, I don't know what. Must be doing pretty well to buy that place and run a couple of expensive cars. She seemed a bit edgy—she'd cut her arm and was all bound up. Did it mending a door hinge or something."

"What about the dog? Could he have got hold of some poison?" Patrick asked. "There's a lot of yew about the place, isn't there?"

"Yes, but I doubt if a dog would eat it, unless some got into his food by accident."

"What effect would it have? Would it cause some sort of coma?"

"I'd expect vomiting and diarrhoea first," said Paul.

Patrick had seen no trace of any of these troubles near the body of the dog.

"What about rat poison?"

"A big dog like that would need to swallow a lot to be fatally affected," Paul said. "And anything with strychnine in it would cause convulsions. He must have had a weak heart, I suppose. After all, animals do, just like people."

Paul Newton seemed set for a long stay in the pub. The bar was filling up now, and Fred Brown's daughter had appeared to help her father. Patrick excused himself and left. As he went round the side of the building to collect his car a red mini came fast down the lane, scattering water from the puddles that had formed since it had rained earlier in the day. It must be Valerie. Though Ellen sometimes borrowed the car, she would never drive like that.

All the same, at the village telephone box Patrick stopped and dialled Ellen's number. This time she answered promptly. He told her that he had booked her room at the Randolph for the next weekend and said he would meet her at the station if she would let him know which train she would be on. She promised to send a postcard, thanked him, and seemed anxious to end the conversation. Patrick knew she was not alone, and just as certainly he was sure that David Bruce, known not to be in Meldsmead that evening, was with her.

He stopped at the garage, which was still open, and filled up with petrol. The owner was chatty. Patrick discovered that he did the maintenance for almost everyone in the village. They talked for some minutes and then Patrick drove up the lane to the vicarage. Mr. Merry had suggested he should call when he was in Meldsmead; it was to be hoped that tonight was no Mother's Union night, or the time appointed for Confirmation class.

It was not. Mr. Merry himself opened the door and recognised Patrick at once.

"Come in, come in," he cried warmly, and called over his shoulder, "Meg, my dear, we have a most welcome visitor."

His wife appeared almost immediately beside him small, smiling, rather like him, the very personification of her name. A most appetising smell was coming from the inner regions of the house, and Patrick, who fully intended to cadge a meal if invited, nevertheless felt shame as the vicar introduced them.

"What a terrible time to call," he said. "You're about to have dinner."

"You shall share it, you shall share it," said Mr. Merry. "Meg had only just said that we should go out into the byways and pluck someone in, as we had an abundance. We were going to pluck Paul Newton, in fact; he's sure to be in the Meldsmead Arms, but here are you, delivered up instead."

"We'd invited Carol Bruce, but she isn't well and can't come. We've plenty of food," beamed Mrs. Merry.

Patrick needed no more urging. They all had a glass of sherry. "Gift of Paul Newton—a most generous man," said the vicar, and Patrick was told again about his sad situation.

"He blames himself for his wife's death," said Mr. Merry. "He's rather a perfectionist—very neat about the house, likes old furniture and good food, and is a connoisseur of wine—hence this excellent sherry. His wife was rather a slapdash soul—charming, but she couldn't achieve the polish she thought he wanted from her. She was untidy, and very unpunctual. She was driving home much too fast from visiting some friend or other when she was killed—hurrying home to get Paul's dinner."

"How tragic," Patrick said. For how many years would Paul carry his burden of guilt? And perhaps they had parted for the last time on a tiff; what a terrible thing to reach the end without a chance to make amends. "He has a family, hasn't he?"

"Yes. A very nice daughter who's pony mad at the moment, and a boy who's a medical student, but I gather is thinking of giving it up," said Mrs. Merry.

"Is he?" The vicar looked surprised.

His wife nodded.

"Yes. Paul's very worried about it."

"He hasn't mentioned it to me," said the vicar.

"He will. He doesn't know what to do; it may be just a whim, or it may go deep," said Meg Merry.

"Did the boy really want to do medicine, or was he pushed into his father's footsteps?" Patrick asked.

"I think he was still hesitating when his mother died. Then he made up his mind," said the vicar.

"You mean he may have felt one blow was enough for his father—he couldn't disappoint him after that happened?" Patrick said.

"I'm afraid it may have been something like that. I did wonder at the time," said Mr. Merry. "But he's passed all his exams and done quite well so far."

"Lionel was very good with Paul after his wife died," Mrs. Merry told Patrick as they went into the dining-room. "You know the sort of thing—the funeral details, and so on, and they spent hours and hours talking together. Paul was always good to us, but he's been even more generous since then. Never comes to church, though."

"She's buried here?"

"She was cremated, but we had the service here first. She was a faithful member of the church; she had a lovely voice. She was always late, though." Meg smiled at the memory.

Dinner was excellent—home-made soup, roast loin of lamb, and peach flan, with a mellow Beaujolais, another gift from Paul Newton.

"I suppose in a village as small as this it's still possible for everyone to know each other," Patrick said. "Where my sister lives, although it's still a village and not a town, it's too large for that. There are whole sections of the community who never meet unless they're involved in some joint activity." Jane, he knew, had met most of her friends through the play group where Andrew spent two mornings a week.

"We are growing," Meg said. "Some of the newer arrivals in the village don't mingle much. Lionel always calls when anyone fresh comes, but they're afraid he's going to start praying over them or something, so they regard him with suspicion. But of course that's a generalisation. It doesn't apply to everyone. Some of the newcomers are much more community-minded than people who've lived here for years."

"I've met the Bruces. They're new, aren't they? You said Mrs. Bruce is ill," Patrick said.

"Oh yes. Poor thing, she's been most unlucky since they moved in. I had quite a shock when I went to see her yesterday," said Mrs. Merry.

Patrick was told once more the story of the doctor's car being seen approaching Abbot's Lodge.

"There she was, in a huge four-poster bed in the room where poor Hesther died, looking just like Hesther, except for the hair. Hesther's was long, and when she was ill she braided it. Carol wears hers quite short. She'd been sick and had an awful headache. Fortunately I was able to fetch the prescription the doctor ordered for her," said Mrs. Merry.

"She's better today though, isn't she, dear?" asked the vicar.

"Yes, much. She must have picked up some germ, or eaten something that disagreed with her."

"I suppose David can cook for himself and look after her. Most men can, these days," said the vicar.

"Well, he'd have been all right last night. I made Carol some tea, and naturally looked into the fridge when I got the milk. There were some chops in it, and some blackberry and apple pie. The pie was still there when I went up this morning though the chops were gone."

"Perhaps David doesn't like blackberry and apple pie," suggested the vicar.

"Would Carol make it, then? Surely not," Mrs. Merry said. "Anyway, it had gone this afternoon. Carol must have decided to throw it away. She's certainly not up to eating it herself—she's still at the bread-and-milk stage. She's not really up—just pottering about in a dressing-gown."

They went on to talk of other things, and some time later, after what had been a very pleasant evening, Patrick took his leave, making a mental resolution to invite them to some Oxford gathering that might be of interest to them.

He was very fond of his white Rover, but tonight he began to wish he owned a car that was a less conspicuous colour. He took the loop road that led away from the village and by which, he supposed, you could eventually find your way towards Basinstoke. After travelling half a mile or so out of the village he pulled into a gateway, hoping that the ground, though wet, was still firm enough to support the weight of the car without the tyres sinking into it, and by the feeble glow of the interior light he studied an ordnance map of the area. This showed that there was a footpath from the lane where he was now, across the fields to the bridge over the stream where he and Ellen had found the body of Rufus. Could he, he wondered, find his way along this route in the dark and the wet? He could not risk meeting any of his new acquaintances by going through the village past Mulberry Cottage down to Abbot's Lodge, especially as Valerie was here for the night. Well, at least he could try this cross-country venture. Thank heaven for a country-dwelling sister, he thought, getting his gumboots out of the car and putting them on. He tucked his trouser ends well in and set off, torch in hand.

The rain had stopped, and a fitful moon appeared now and then through the clouds. Patrick found the stile that marked the start of his journey, climbed it, and embarked across the very soggy field, hoping he was heading in the right direction. Rustlings and grunts in the field indicated the presence of beasts; he made out the dark humps of them in the brief moments when the moon shone: steers, he supposed. He did not want to shine his torch; there was no explanation he could possibly give for his presence here, if challenged. On he blundered, guided by the intermittent shafts of moonlight that filtered past the mass of nimbus in the sky, and at length he met the stream. He had only to follow it now to reach the bridge, and this was easy enough, though there were several wire fences to cross. But his legs were long and he stepped over them easily. He came to the bridge, crossed it, then went on to the hedge that bounded the grounds of Abbot's Lodge. This was the way he had walked with Ellen. Tonight he did not open the gate that led into the garden; he could see a light burning in an upstairs window: Carol's bedroom, where she lay in her four-poster recovering from her malaise. He skirted round the hedge and slipped in through the main gate. Here he risked a brief flash from the torch and soon saw the dustbin by the back door. It was one of a kind issued by many councils now, a solid wire frame with a hinged lid, with a plastic bag attached ready for neat removel by the refuse disposal men. Because the lid was made of rubber he was able to raise it silently and examine the contents; he had to shine his torch, but he quickly found a newspaper parcel containing a large slice of blackberry and apple pie. With his penknife he shaved off a thin sliver, put it in an old envelope he had in his pocket, wrapped up the parcel again and restored it to the squalid interior of the dustbin. Then he set off on the return journey back to his car by the way he had come.

This time he glanced at Mulberry Cottage as he walked along beside the stream. There he had consoled Ellen about the dog's death only five days before while they listened to Verdi on her transistor radio. Now all was dark. Valerie must keep early hours.

He had acquired several pounds of mud on either boot by the time he reached his car again, but his eyes had grown used to the darkness and the return journey was easier than the outward one. It was lucky there were cattle in the fields, whose hoofmarks would obliterate his tracks. He hoped he had left no traces of mud around the yard at Abbot's Lodge.

As he drove back to Oxford he reflected on the lucky chance that decreed Meldsmead's dustbins should not be emptied on Thursdays. He managed to banish from his mind the conviction that David Bruce was with Ellen in her flat until he had wrapped up and labelled the slice of blackberry and apple pie neatly, ready to give it to a friend of his the next day to be analysed.

PART FIVE

"I can't get this business of the dog out of my mind," said Patrick. It was the following Sunday evening, and he had spent the day with Jane and Michael. Young Andrew was in bed, and they had just had soup, cold pork, baked potatoes and salad, and cherry flan, sitting by a log fire in the living-room. "Mike, you'll be portly when you're middle-aged if Jane feeds you like this."

"I'm getting portly already," Michael said, though in fact he was not.

"Think of all those poor lonely dons' wives with their tomato soup on their trays and the Sunday film on the box, while their husbands dine in hall. What a dreary life," said Jane.

"I wouldn't dine in hall on Sundays if I was married," said Patrick. "Notice that I'm not there now."

"You would if you had four argumentative brats," said Michael. He grinned at Jane. "We haven't reached that stage. It's still peaceful when you can make them doss down at a suitable hour."

"How's my niece?" asked Patrick.

Jane patted her stomach.

"Active," she said.

"There are too many aunts and nieces in this whole

affair," said Patrick. "Old Amelia and her niece Valerie, and then Ellen."

"Yes, Ellen," said Jane and exchanged a glance with Michael.

"Why is all this so much on your mind, Patrick?" Michael asked. In the past Patrick's fantastic speculations and theories had proved to be not as far-fetched as they seemed at first, and he had a great respect for his brother-in-law's judgment, but he thought him insulated from reality, tucked away in his academic fastness among the dreaming spires. "After all, life is full of inexplicable things and strange happenings."

"I know it is. But two old ladies, two respected spinsters, die suddenly, within a couple of months of one another, both by falling down rather special stairs, and both were friends. Then a dog drowns."

"O.K. So the two old girls fell down the stairs. That's an odd coincidence, I'll allow you that. But you saw the first old lady fall yourself, and knew it was an accident. The second old lady was depressed and sad, perhaps, and she had a weak heart. Delayed shock may have caused her death. Anyway, what a splendid way to die."

"Falling down the stairs in the British Museum? I can't agree," said Patrick.

"I really meant the suddenness of it, and the other one, the one who died on the Acropolis," said Michael.

"It wasn't splendid, Michael," Patrick said. Once again he saw the thin limbs crudely exposed, and the shocked Greek policeman swiftly covering them.

"But there can't be any connection with the dog. Maybe he had a weak heart too."

"Another coincidence? Maybe."

Patrick did not want to tell them about Ellen and David. To say it aloud would be to force himself to admit it. The first time he had seen them together, in the field, could have been innocent, but there was no mistake about the way they had looked at one another that morning in the British Museum. Circumstantial evidence, he told himself sternly, unsupported by the facts needed for the true researcher.

"I went to Meldsmead on Thursday," he said abruptly. "I hadn't got the feel of the village—I wanted to try to sense the atmosphere. I had a drink in the pub and met a man there whom I'd spoken to before. He told me Carol Bruce had been ill. Some sort of stomach upset."

"Gastric flu. There's a lot about," said Jane.

"Or else there is some sort of curse on that house, as everybody says. Ellen thinks so," he said.

"Patrick, just what are you afraid of?" Jane demanded, putting down her knitting and looking at him. "You don't really want to go on with this, do you? Yet usually you're looking for mysteries in the most normal events. Are you afraid that Ellen is involved in something sinister? Do you think the dog was killed on purpose, as a warning, perhaps?"

"I think that someone doesn't want Carol Bruce at Abbot's Lodge," said Patrick. "She put her foot through the floorboards of a room that had been re-floored. She slipped on some steps that were perfectly dry except for where I found a trace of fine oil. She scratched her arm doing a household repair, and her dog has died mysteriously. And now she's ill. Oh, and her car had a puncture."

"She's just accident-prone," said Jane. "And people do have punctures all the time, even with tubeless tyres."

"I went to the garage at Meldsmead on Thursday for some petrol, and got talking to the owner. Carol's so-called puncture wasn't one. There was no trace of a hole in it when the wheel was brought in for repair. It must have been let down. Deliberately, I mean."

"How? Couldn't it have been the valve?" Michael asked.

"The flat tyre was found after the Bruces had been out to a party. It was completely flat—right down on the rim. It couldn't have been just a leaky valve—that would have gone down slowly and might have taken twenty-four hours or more to lose all its air."

"Some hooligan boys let it down," Jane said promptly.

"In a remote lane, well away from the village? Where there's no other house, just the Bradshaws' market garden?"

"Certainly the car couldn't have been driven on a really flat tyre without it being noticed," Michael said. "Who did spot it?"

"David. He was going to drive it home, but he noticed the car sagging—you know how they do when one tyre is really down. They had no pump and he changed the wheel."

"But this is fanciful in the extreme. Why should anyone want to get Carol Bruce to leave Abbot's Lodge?" Michael demanded.

"It's been empty for ages. Maybe some gang had got it earmarked as a hideout. Maybe something is hidden there—thieves do dump stuff and collect it later, even after years, when they come out of gaol," said Jane.

"Well, all right let's accept that, however unlikely it seems, as some sort of reason. It still doesn't connect up with your old ladies," said Michael.

"Supposing we could find a link?" Patrick said.

"There can't be one."

"There's Meldsmead."

"Do you believe that Miss Amelia saw someone like the train robbers hiding their loot at Abbot's Lodge and they did her in? Nonsense," said Jane. "If there was anything odd going on there and she knew about it, she'd report it at once—her duty, you know. Don't forget the Slade House motto—'Virtue in all I do'."

"No. Miss Amelia's death was an accident. That youth jostled her and she fell. It could have happened to any old lady who happened to be standing where she was at that moment. It was her own fault for not being in a better position. She happened to be standing above a sheer drop—short, but sheer. She fell and bowled down the stairs below. A younger person would have retrieved their balance somehow—clutched at someone, maybe had a broken leg, but might not have been killed."

"She hadn't found some ancient archaeological prize she was about to smuggle back to England in her reticule?" suggested Michael.

"If she'd found an archaeological gem she'd have handed it over at once to some authority," said Jane.

"So she wasn't running up faked amphorae in the cellar of Abbot's Lodge either. It's not her ghost haunting Carol," Michael said.

"Why don't you forget it, Patrick?" Jane said. "It's making you unhappy. Usually you're all animated when you're on the trail of something. You're wrong this time, surely, aren't you? It's just a chapter of rather unhappy accidents. The next thing you hear, Carol will be full of beans and it will all be forgotten. The broken floorboard was probably dishonest workmen—maybe they replaced the worst bits and the previous owners paid for the whole thing, all unbeknownst."

"You could be right," said Patrick. "I think I'll take your advice. Anyway, I've a lot on next week. I'll calm down unless someone else falls down some stairs." Or until he had the result of the tests on the blackberry pie.

And next week Ellen was coming to Oxford.

Would she still come, or would she stand him up?

11

She did come. He met her at the station on Saturday afternoon, took her to the Randolph, parking right outside on the double yellow line in defiance of the traffic warden patrolling nearby, and saw her into the hotel. As she was led off to her room he arranged to pick her up at half-past six. Then he drove back to St. Mark's and after he had bathed, shaved, and changed himself he spent the remaining interval until it was time to fetch her fussing round his sitting-room, moving chairs and cushions fractionally, and adjusting the flowers which to Robert, his scout's, astonishment he had brought that morning. Patrick had often entertained women in his room but Robert could never remember flowers being brought in to embellish the surroundings before.

She was coming down the staircase into the hall of the hotel as he arrived. She wore a plain black velvet dress with long sleeves and a high round neck; her only jewellery was a pair of drop earrings, garnets set with pearls. So this is what the poets meant, thought Patrick as he floated through the air towards her, managing to forget David Bruce for ten whole seconds.

"You look wonderful," he said, unable to think of anything less mundane to say.

"I thought this would be suitable," she answered, with the demure smile that enchanted him. He looked pretty good himself, she thought; he was tall, and sturdily built, and behind his large-rimmed glasses his eyes looked steadily into her. He had a determined chin, but his mouth was wide and gentle-looking; it was a strong face, the face of a man who would make up his mind and stick to his decision, a man who might be stubborn but who was certainly sensitive and perceptive. For once his fine, dark hair was not flopping over his forehead but brushed smoothly back; she had met him often enough now to know that it would soon fall forward.

She was carrying her coat. He helped her into it, took her by the elbow and led her out to the car. Then he whisked her by small side roads to St. Mark's, where it lurked in obscurity at the end of a cobbled street, one of Oxford's smallest and oldest colleges.

"I don't know Oxford at all well," she said, as they went along. "I've just passed through a few times. Now one doesn't even do that, with the ring road. I know the other place better. Isn't that what you call it?"

He laughed.

"That's right," he said. "Here we are." He turned into

the wide gateway leading into the first quadrangle. "Parking laid on and everything."

"I knew dons led sheltered lives," said Ellen.

"We do as regards parking, that's certain," Patrick said. "But we come up against stark facts now and then. Our young men have their problems, and so do we. This way."

He took her through the main quad and into a smaller one beyond it, then to the staircase that led to his rooms.

"It's quite a climb, but worth it when you get there," he said. "We've time for a quick drink before we go down."

His efforts to arrange his decanters and heavy Waterford tumblers to best effect, were successful. Her rapturous appreciation of where he lived was quite spontaneous.

"Patrick! What a beautiful room! Look at all your books—and what lovely curtains—and the pictures!" She flitted round, inspecting and exclaiming, and he stood like a tongue-tied boy admiring her until at last his social sense released his paralysis, and he dealt with their drinks.

They sat sedately on either side of the fireplace drinking sherry, which was what Ellen had chosen, and he told her about his fellow dons whom she would meet later.

"I hope I won't disgrace you," she said.

"On the contrary, you'll make everyone regard me with envy and new respect," he said.

"I will sit next to you, won't I?" she asked anxiously. "I haven't been to anything like this before."

"Oh yes. And on your other side will be Bernard Wilson, the librarian, so you can talk about your great-aunt's books to him. He's an amiable chap—looks a bit unusual, but dons often do."

"I'll try not to stare at him," said Ellen, smiling.

Just before half-past seven they went down to the Senior Common Room, where Ellen was introduced with due formality to the Master and his wife. The

Master turned out to be a white-haired man of about sixty who did not seem in the least formidable, and his wife, who wore a curious dress of what looked like homespun tweed, had a round face innocent of any make-up, and large guileless blue eyes so that it was impossible to feel awed by her. Bernard Wilson certainly did look rather odd with his thick pebble glasses and heavy beard, but he was so pleased to meet the great-great niece, as they worked out she must be, of the celebrated E. C. Brinton whose contributions to classical scholarship had been so great, that any shyness Ellen felt was soon dispelled. Patrick saw that she had relaxed and was preparing to enjoy herself.

Ellen found it was quite an experience to be seated at the High Table facing a sea of youthful faces ranged at right angles below. An undergraduate with flowing but clean locks read a Latin grace and the meal began. The speed with which it was consumed astounded Ellen; in no time at all, it seemed to her, the hall was clear of young men, and even at the High Table plates were removed with startling rapidity. Half her orange soufflé disappeared when she laid down her fork for a moment to answer some remark of Bernard Wilson's.

After the pudding course, the members of the S.C.R. and their guests returned to the Senior Common Room for dessert. Port and madeira circled round, and this time everyone sat another way, with the don next in seniority to the Master presiding. This was Bernard Wilson. His guest, a woman don who often appeared on television and wrote learned books on prehistory, sat beside him. Ellen now found herself augustly placed beside the Master. He enquired where she lived and what she did, and talked about his married daughter in Vancouver, where he hoped to go in the long vacation. Ellen had spent a year in Canada after her secretarial training and had worked her way across to the West Coast. They talked about totem poles, and how to read the legends they told, and the problem of the Indians. Time flew, and eventually the Master and his wife left, followed by some of the other guests. Those remaining changed their seats again in another bout of General Post and began to talk shop of various sorts. Ellen was fascinated; she had never spent an evening like it, and what impressed her most was the extreme courtesy of everyone. At each introduction a potted biography of either party was related to the other so that there was some starting point for conversation, and everyone talked as if they really were interested in what they were saying, and the responses their remarks evoked. She was encouraged to talk about her own job, and learned that most of the married dons, particularly the younger ones, lived in college-owned flats or houses. The world of commerce in which she moved was alien here, Ellen realised a little bleakly.

After a while Bernard Wilson suggested that she and Patrick should join him and his guest in his rooms for a nightcap. They wound their way there along tortuous passages and up and down various flights of stairs. Over the doorway the legend *Dr. B. L. Wilson* was neatly painted in white. Patrick's door had been similarly labelled with his name. That was the only resemblance between the two sets, for the interior of Bernard's was chaotic. There were books and papers piled on every chair and heaped all over the floor, so that spaces had to be cleared among them before anyone could sit down. Then there was a hunt for four glasses of any sort, let alone matching ones. But the drink cupboard was well-stocked. The Burmanns, which Patrick had brought back from Mulberry Cottage were displayed to Ellen, proudly shelved in a glass-fronted cupboard, and Bernard told her he was eager to buy many more of Amelia's collection, including, on behalf of a pupil, her Oxford edition of Cicero.

"One volume's missing," Ellen said.

"Has it not turned up?" Patrick asked. "It will. I'm sure. It must have got into the wrong place somehow."

Bernard's guest had taken off her shoes which she said pinched her toes. She padded about the room in bare feet picking up papers and inspecting them, then casting them from her in a despairing way. After that she fell to bemoaning the intellectual levels of her pupils and declared that none would get any sort of degree, much less good ones.

Later, Patrick told Ellen that this woman was a brilliant teacher and one of the best brains in the university, but drinking made her melancholy.

"And she has a rare virtue. She isn't afraid of being outclassed by her pupils—she welcomes any challenge," he added.

Ellen digested this information as they trekked back through the building to his rooms, where she had left her coat.

"Don't you ever leave papers about?" she asked him, looking at its orderly state.

"Often. But I tidied up for you. I wanted to create a good impression," he said. "Have I managed it?"

"Yes, you have," she said. "How nice they are, all your colleagues. Their manners are so marvellous. People push and shove so, in London. It's restful to be somewhere where there's ritual in what goes on."

"Customs and ceremonies have their merits," Patrick agreed. "But dons can be pretty beastly to one another, when aroused. Many are the feuds among us. Have you enjoyed your evening?"

"Very much," she said, and meant it.

III

In the morning Patrick showed her the college by daylight, and they spent some time in the library. Ellen was intrigued by the ancient volumes still chained in place as they had been centuries before. Then she said she must go down to Mulberry Cottage and was there a bus?

"I'll take you," he said.

"Oh no, Patrick. I couldn't put you to all that trouble," she replied.

"Nonsense," he said. "It's no trouble." Just a very great pity and dire disappointment; he had planned a day in the Cotswolds and then a return to Mark's for tea in his room.

She softened the blow a little.

"We could look out a few more of those books Dr. Wilson wanted, perhaps," she suggested. "There'll be something we can eat. I'm sure, even if it's only a tin."

He brightened. She had not, then, got an assignation in the meadows with David.

She was wearing her blackberry-coloured trouser suit and her hair was freed from its usual clasp, so that it hung loose on her shoulders. It made her look very young. As they drove off Patrick was silent. Having successfully banished all thought of David Bruce from his mind for hours, now he could not get rid of it; old-fashioned sentiments on the lines of how dare he trifle with her rushed through his head, and were followed by the notion that it might not be just trifling. Ellen sensed the tension in him, and could only think of trite remarks to make about the landscape as they passed. The easy feeling there had been between them had disappeared and she began to regret that they were committed to spending a good part of the day together.

There were a number of cars parked outside the Meldsmead Arms.

"Shall I nip in and get us some beer? Or would you like to have a drink here?" Patrick asked.

"Let's take some back with us," Ellen said.

"Right." Patrick stopped the car and got out. "Won't be long," he said.

Both bars were busy but Fred Brown had time to greet him at once. He bought four pints of light ale. That should do for today and for some future occasion when Ellen entertained David Bruce, he thought bitterly. Perhaps this evening, after he had gone, David would come to visit her.

He pulled himself together as he went back to the car; what had happened to his obedient mind that it was wandering along such profitless paths?

Ellen picked up various letters from just inside the front door before they stepped inside. Patrick's sharp eye noticed the electricity bill and what looked like a rates demand. There was one letter without a stamp which she stuffed quickly into her pocket; the rest she laid on the table in the sitting-room. One large envelope was addressed to Miss Amelia and came from some classical society to which she had belonged.

"Their computer doesn't seem to have caught up with things," said Ellen. She opened the window. "It smells stuffy, doesn't it, yet it's cold."

"Shall I light the fire?" said Patrick. It would give him some occupation while Ellen foraged for lunch, and take his mind off his churning thoughts.

"Oh, what a good idea. There are sticks and things in the shed."

Patrick went off on his errand. In the shed, which was at the rear of the cottage, he found kindling and some logs. There didn't seem to be any coal. There was a tin of paraffin and another of creosote, various garden tools, and a pile of old papers and magazines which he thought would be too damp to ignite with any ease. He collected up a load of twigs and logs, found some dry newspaper in the kitchen, and soon had a promising fire going in the big hearth. It smoked a little at first, but as the wood caught and the chill left the chimney it drew better. He piled on logs and went in search of Ellen, who had disappeared.

He saw her from the kitchen window. She was at the far end of the garden near the fence by the field, reading a letter, the one she had so swiftly pocketed when they arrived, no doubt. She had taken off her jacket, and with her hair loose she looked almost like a boy as she came back towards the cottage, walking slowly, looking at the ground.

As soon as she came indoors the illusion was dispelled; she was utterly feminine. She produced a large tin of curry and cooked some rice. With this, and fresh apples from the garden, and the beer, they had an excellent meal. Then they found the Cicero *Letters* for Bernard; Ellen said the *Orations* must wait until the missing one was found. Finally Patrick felt obliged to leave, and Ellen did not press him to stay. She had a date, he thought in fury.

But she thanked him with every appearance of sincerity for the evening at Mark's, and for bringing her back to Meldsmead.

"How will you get back to London?" he could not resist enquiring, rubbing salt into his already smarting wound.

"Oh, I'll get the early train tomorrow. George Kent commutes. He'll take me to the station," she said. She did not mention David, who probably went up each day on the motorway in his BMW.

Patrick drove off, moving rapidly up through the gears to get away quickly, since it had to happen. Watching him out of sight, Ellen felt suddenly forlorn; it came to her that she was letting go something of great value that might never come her way again.

PART SIX

Jane was definitely plumper. She had acquired a placid look, and was knitting.

"You do look cow-like," Patrick said.

"Thanks very much."

"Must be strange," he mused.

"It's quite often rather uncomfortable, but it's gratifying. I feel smug and docile," Jane said.

They sat in silence for a while, while Patrick meditated and Jane knitted calmly on. Michael was away at a conference and he had come to spend the evening. At last Jane said, after casting several shrewd glances at him:

"Patrick, something's eating you. What is it? Wasn't the weekend a success?" For she had known that Ellen was coming to Oxford.

"It was wonderful. She's a marvellous girl with a good brain—she doesn't realise herself how good it is—and she's pretty and gentle—" his voice trailed off and he looked somewhat embarrassed.

Jane was amazed at this extravagant speech.

"Well then, why don't you bring her over here some time?" she said, pretending to count her stitches.

"She's messing about with David Bruce. That's the chap with the haunted house and the dead dog."

"How do you know she is?"

"I've seen them together," he said. He recounted his experience in the British Museum. "I'd meant to ask her out to lunch," he said. "But there wasn't any point. There was no doubt about the situation between them —if you'd seen how they looked at one another—"

"Why were you prowling round among the marbles?" Jane asked.

"I was casing the joint. I wanted to see if someone could push an old lady down the stairs and vanish upwards," Patrick said.

"And could it be done?"

"Easily."

"But that didn't happen. It would have been seen. You can't go pushing people down stairs and running off. A witness would collar you."

"Someone you knew, if you were an old lady, could take your arm and then suddenly shove you, when no one seemed to be looking," Patrick said.

"Not Ellen! Why should she want to get rid of poor Mildred Forrest?" Jane exclaimed.

"No. Why should she? But someone else might."

"Who?"

"I can't think. She must have been utterly harmless," Patrick said. "I'm imagining things again."

Could Miss Forrest have stumbled on the truth of the relationship between Ellen and David, and bidden her to the museum to chide her? She might have felt it her duty, as Miss Amelia's friend. Or if not to chide, to advise?

"Jane—all that stuff about the Slade House motto —virtue is my breastplate or whatever you said it was —what would Miss Amelia have thought about goings-on by any of her girls?"

"Do you mean what would she have thought about adulterous associations?" asked Jane firmly.

"Well—yes."

"She would have been slow to accept that any of her girls could indulge in such acts," Jane said. "But once convinced, or if she should learn that any of her girls had done anything else she deplored, she'd do her best to expunge them from her memory. It would be as if they'd never existed."

"Now? In the nineteen-seventies?"

"Very much so. She'd go on till the very last moment believing the best of everyone, and she'd admit that her own code was strict, but if someone she'd had influence over didn't live up to her standards she'd think it her own failure."

"You're sure of all this? She left before you went there, remember."

"Thank goodness she did. She must have been a tartar," Jane said. "But it was part of the Slade House legend, handed down as the lore of the past."

"Hm" Patrick grunted.

"I don't see what you're getting at."

"I don't see it myself. I'm thinking aloud, really." Patrick rootled in his pocket and pulled out a dried seed pod; he ferreted about in the depths near the seam and found some actual seeds, small and black. "Do you know what these are?" he asked.

Jane looked at them.

"Laburnum seeds, aren't they?"

"Yes. Very poisonous. I got them from the Bruce's garden."

"And?"

"The dog died. Carol Bruce was sick."

"You're not suggesting someone fed them both laburnum seeds?"

"There's a yew hedge, too, round the house. That's also poisonous," Patrick said.

"Patrick, no. People don't go round murdering their wives just because they fancy someone else. They get divorced, or have affairs," said Jane.

"David Bruce may not have wanted a divorce," Patrick said. "His wife may have a lot of money. She's certainly got expensive tastes. And Ellen isn't the sort of girl to be happy just being someone's mistress indefinitely."

He could not now ask Ellen whether it was Carol who had bought the house; he knew that it was she who had wanted it, much more than David. But then again, he had only Ellen's word for that. What if it were David who had decided on the house?

"Leave it, leave it, Patrick," Jane urged him. "Wait a year. Keep away from Ellen and find someone else, or if you can't do that, at least stop looking for mysteries. Ellen will get over David in a year, if she's as you say she is. Then, if you still find her special, try again."

The thought that this wretched girl preferred anyone to her brother was anathema to Jane.

"Oh, I'm not smitten," Patrick said lightly. "She's just different—one on her own."

Jane was not deceived.

"And I can't leave it alone. Something's wrong, but I don't know what it is. A dog has died. An innocent woman keeps having accidents, and two old ladies have fallen to their deaths."

"We'll accept that Ellen and David are having an affair," said Jane. "What possible link can that have with Amelia?"

"She wouldn't have approved."

"She didn't know about it. She was dead before the Bruces came to Meldsmead. And if she's doing a haunt, it would be David she'd be badgering, or Ellen, not Carol." Jane had abandoned her knitting now and was gazing at him earnestly. "Patrick dear, do leave it. This time it's you that will get hurt," she said.

"I'm afraid I'm hurt already," Patrick admitted. "I can't leave it. I'm so sure something else dreadful is going to happen. You can't just walk away from things because they're unpleasant. That doesn't make them vanish."

Jane had often heard Patrick hold forth the sin of indifference.

"What's this David like?" she asked.

"Oh—all right, I suppose. I'd dislike him whatever he was like in fact," said Patrick. "He was a bit hopeless about the dog—the burying of it, and all that. I was surprised he didn't want a post-mortem, to know why it had died." If he'd poisoned it, of course he wouldn't want the fact disclosed. "The wife's the stronger character."

"Why are you so sure of that? You've only met her once, haven't you?"

It was true.

"I don't know. Perhaps I felt that David was weak, and two weak people don't get married to each other."

"Oh Patrick, yes they do. They flutter happily together in perfect harmony," said Jane, laughing at him. "I think you're biased against David. He may be perfectly delightful."

"Maybe he's loaded to the gills with sex appeal," said Patrick gloomily.

"Well, so are you, so you should worry," Jane declared, and saw him turn a deep crimson shade.

"I know. I've seen the effect you have on women," she declared. "Otherwise I couldn't tell you so—it's not an aspect of their brothers that sisters take much heed of and can judge."

"Michael sometimes cooks the supper, doesn't he?" he said, abruptly changing the subject.

"Yes. When he's in the mood. Why?"

"Does he make things like pies? Blackberry and apple, that sort of thing?"

Jane stared.

"Good heavens, no. He makes jolly good meat dishes but never a pud—and before we were married, when he was busy seducing girls in his flat, he used to buy ready-made pavlovas and what-not from a patisserie nearby. Lots of people buy ready-made puddings."

"Oh. That's a useful bit of information you've given me," Patrick said.

"Any time," said Jane, picking up her knitting once again.

The next Wednesday night Patrick went down to Meldsmead once more. He drove through the village, fortunately meeting no one, and parked where he had left the car before his previous walk across the fields. Then, on foot, as on the other occasion, he climbed the stile, but this time he went to Mulberry Cottage. No lights showed: a quick look round revealed no car outside, and the windows were blank, the curtains still drawn back; no one was there. He had no real plan, just the feeling that some key to what was troubling him lay here, if he could only find it.

The front and back doors were both securely locked, and all the windows were tightly closed. He could not get in. He did not know what he expected to find, just something to trigger his mind in a new direction. He went into the shed where he had found the kindling wood on Sunday. There was the pile of papers and magazines, stacked on a shelf. He could use his torch freely in here without fear of being seen, and he took them down, careful not to disturb the dust and bird droppings from the top copy of *The Times*. It was, he saw, three years old. He lifted it carefully off. Below were copies of *Punch*, *The Illustrated London News*, and then, wrapped between two venerable copies of the *Sunday Times*, he found a photograph album. It was old and spotted with damp; some of the photographs were yellow and some had stuck together. It seemed to consist wholly of groups of schoolgirls. He wrapped it up again, separated it from its pile, and then replaced the other papers where he had found them.

II

"If I were a policeman, it would be so easy to find out all the things I want to know," said Patrick.

It was the following afternoon, and he was back with Jane. Andrew had gone out to tea with a small boy who lived nearby.

"Won't your pal at Scotland Yard do it for you? He has before, I seem to remember."

"We haven't got a body this time. We had then."

"I thought you just had a missing person the last time you started rooting around. You didn't wait for the body to turn up."

"No one's missing now."

"No. And no one's acting suspiciously. One dog had died in mysterious circumstances, that's all. What do you want to find out?"

"What sort of people they all are. How much money they have, what they want from life—all that."

"Who specially?"

"Oh, the Bruces. And Ellen, I suppose." He looked bleak. "And everyone else in the village. I went back there last night."

"Whatever for?" Jane stared.

"I don't know. Some odd compulsion. I'm still worried about my old ladies."

"What happened last night, then?"

"Absolutely nothing, except that I found this." He prodded his newspaper parcel. "It's an album of Slade House photographs. It was in the shed at Mulberry Cottage buried under some old newspapers and magazines. It's pretty ancient. Is there the slightest chance that you'd recognise anyone? I've looked through them myself but they're meaningless to me."

He wanted to wipe out all possibility of Ellen being involved in any scheme to harm Carol Bruce. She could not be a party to any such act, and if David were in any way wanting to threaten his wife, the sooner he was exposed and Ellen disillusioned the better.

"Let's have a look," said Jane. "You'd recognise Valerie, wouldn't you? But people change so. I hope I've improved since then."

"Valerie didn't go there. She was educated abroad somewhere," Patrick said. "It's rather grubby," he warned, handing her the album.

"Hm. Sniffs a bit, doesn't it? Why on earth was it in the shed?"

"I can't imagine. Perhaps it got thrown out by mistake."

"Maybe Valerie put it out there meaning to give it to the dustmen. She must have done a lot of sorting after Amelia died."

"I don't think she's got around to much of it yet. I expect she had to wait for valuers and things, for probate, and apart from the books I doubt if anything else has been done. Miss Amelia must have been a pretty orderly sort of person, I shouldn't think she left a muddle."

Jane turned the first page. Some schoolgirls in gymslips looked at her with plain round faces. "They all look alike," she said. "Plaits prevail, don't they? Funny how fashions come back and we're long-haired again now." She scrutinised the faded prints. "So you want to know about the Bruces, do you? You think friend David married Carol for her lolly and that's why he won't leave her and run off with your Ellen."

"She's not my Ellen. But why doesn't he? And why move to the very village where Ellen has connections?"

"Try to stay objective, ducky," Jane advised. "He may not have been entangled with Ellen, when he bought the house—it doesn't take long to start an affair, after all."

"Or else it may have been sheer brazen nerve," said Patrick. "Installing himself on her doorstep."

"But he must have begun to negotiate for the house before Amelia died. These things take ages."

"Exactly. And Ellen used to stay with Amelia sometimes. She said the old girl was trying to educate her."

"The old girl would have had something to say if Ellen was carrying on with David in the boskage," Jane remarked. "Look, here's Miss Amelia and Miss Forrest."

Sure enough, there was Miss Amelia, upright and with dark hair; and beside her stood Miss Forrest looking quite plump. Five other women were with them.

"That's surely Miss Chesterfield," said Jane. "Golly, doesn't she look young! We thought her antique. Sofa, we called her, poor thing."

"Who was she?"

Jane pointed out a smiling young woman wearing a blouse and pleated skirt.

"She taught history. She can only have been a girl when this was taken. Look at her smooth cheeks."

Miss Chesterfield did look very young, Patrick agreed.

"Where is she now?" he asked.

"Goodness, I don't know—yes, I do remember what happened to her," Jane said. "She married a parson and went out to some place in Africa. There was a whip-round for her among her former pupils and I coughed up because she taught me a lot and but for her efforts I wouldn't have scraped into our great university."

"Is she still out there?"

"I've no idea. Probably. People get the call and stay in those places for ever, don't they? Or get killed by rebels."

"What bit of Africa? Any idea?"

"None," said Jane tranquilly. "But I expect the Slade House secretary will have a note of her address."

"Will you get it, Jane? Do it tomorrow. Make some excuse. Miss Chesterfield-that-was might be in England now," he said. "I've got a feeling we may need someone who knows about Slade House in Amelia's days."

"Well, most of the old brigade of the staff will be dead, I should think," Jane said. "But probably old Chesterfield's minding lots of little sofas somewhere. I'll see what I can do."

"Do you crack ghastly jokes like that to Michael?" Patrick asked her.

"Sometimes. He thinks I'm very amusing," Jane said.

"I suppose he's got to humour you, in your condition," said Patrick, but he was grinning, which was something, Jane thought, having striven to make him smile. "Thanks. Your Mrs. Sofa would be able to put names to most of the people in this book, wouldn't she?"

"I'm sure she would. But I don't see how that will help."

"Suppose someone in the village had been to Slade House—" he paused. "Miss Amelia would have known them."

"Patrick, are you thinking that there's someone who's photograph may be in this album, who blotted her Slade House copybook so that Miss Amelia chucked the whole thing out—maybe meaning to go through it later but instead left it in the shed?"

"Yes, I am," he said. "But I don't know where that gets us."

"One thing's certain," Jane said, turning another page.

"Oh?"

"These are the bright girls. They're the Sixth Form or the scholarship set—look, some of them are labelled like that. It should help to put names to them. Amelia wouldn't have bothered with the dunderheads. I should think this one, for instance, is the head girl of the day; look at how she's sitting, all busty and proud."

"There'd be records at the school of who was in what form and when?"

"Bound to be. Surely all schools must keep files like

that? But I can't go as far as that for you, Patrick. I'll ask for Chesterfield's address, that's fair enough. The rest will have to wait. If you stumble on anything concrete the police will be able to check."

"If no one else falls down stairs first," said Patrick.

"I can't see why you're so obsessed with this idea," said Jane. "Your steely heart has got itself affected at long last, and it's gone to your brain. You're demented, my poor brother."

"I hope that's all it is," Patrick said heavily. "Jane, there's one other thing you can do for me. You're quite fit now, aren't you?"

"Yes, fine. Just bone idle."

"Are you fit to come with me to Meldsmead, have a noggin at the pub, and if necessary do a fake faint outside the vicarage or some other house?"

"So that we can lawfully get in? Only one house?"

"Well, one to start with."

"The things I do for you," she sighed. "Why?"

"I want you to meet some of the natives. There'll be a few in the pub. We'll play it by ear from there."

"Will I meet the fair Ellen?"

"That's not in my plan," said Patrick.

"Oh. Pity."

"Your female intuition might stumble on something. I've met several husbands but not their wives—something rum may be going on that I haven't thought of."

"Someone other than Ellen fancying David Bruce and putting yew berries in Carol's tea, you mean," Jane said.

"I deplore your phraseology, but that's the general idea," he said. Mrs. Merry had, on her own admission, made tea for Carol, but that was after she was sick. There may have been other ministering angels at work earlier. "I rather favour the idea that Abbot's Lodge could have been used as rendezvous for something or other," Patrick went on.

"My suggestion." Jane preened herself.

"But what? Lovers' meeting? Very uncomfortable in an empty house."

"You could take a li-lo along, I suppose," Jane said. "But wouldn't it be risky, right under the nose of the other spouse?"

"It's so isolated, and so handy. Ideal for brief meetings," Patrick said.

"But mightn't it have been used by a different set of people than those you've met? The young people—ordinary village people?"

"Easily. And I don't see how we'd find that out. But if someone's trying to scare Carol off, it should be possible to find out who it is."

"Only by watching the place night and day," said Jane.

"Even that's not impossible to manage," Patrick said.

"It's like a sort of voodoo thing, isn't it? You'll be finding a wax image of the wretched Carol speared through the middle next," said Jane. "I feel sorry for that girl. Her husband's having an affair with Ellen, and spooks are getting at her almost daily. Do you like her?" She shot the question at him.

"I don't really know," he said slowly. "I've only met her once, and to be quite honest, I was taking more notice of Ellen. She seemed very thrilled with the house—full of plans for improving it. A very efficient woman—strong personality."

"Attractive?"

"Not my type," he said promptly. "But I should think so, yes. Well turned out."

"You didn't see her the day the dog died?"

"No. She drove back after I'd left."

"She's lucky to have one of those Lancias. They cost a bomb," said Jane. "Where had she been that day?"

"Chatting someone up or photographing them for a piece she was writing, I believe," said Patrick.

"Must be keen, working on a Sunday."

"Maybe it was someone not available in the week."

"Maybe it was a dishy man. If David's playing around, why shouldn't she?"

"That's a thought," said Patrick. "Maybe she began it, and that's why David strayed."

"But all this is supposition, Patrick. It's all ifs."

"These things always are. First find a theory, then see if you can prove it," he answered.

"I believe you're afraid that Miss Forrest had found out Ellen was playing around with David, and meant, in the mantle of Miss Amelia, to tell her off, or even threaten to tell Carol, and Ellen pushed her down the stairs, having got the idea because Miss Amelia had died that way," Jane said.

"It would have been physically possible for her to have done it. She could have met Miss Forrest on the landing of the front stairs at the B.M. She could have taken her arm and led her, then shoved her. Miss Forrest would have suspected nothing; Ellen could have rushed on upwards, gone round the building and reappeared in the hall below while all the confusion was still going on."

"She ran the risk of being recognised."

"She could have chosen her moment for pushing Miss Forrest, waiting till no one was around. And she could have worn a mackintosh, and taken it off, or the other way round," said Patrick.

"You don't really believe she did do that, do you? You couldn't have a yen for her if you think her capable of such an awful thing."

"No, I don't believe it."

"But you won't be happy till you've proved it, one way or the other. I see. Hm. Well, by all means let's go to Meldsmead. I'll park Andrew or get a sitter, if it's likely to be a late do. Michael will want to be in on this. I presume you don't want me to hold a torch while you exhume that unfortunate dog?"

"Not this time, no," said Patrick, perfectly seriously. "If it's necessary, Michael and I can manage that on our own."

PART SEVEN

Ellen had tried several times to gain entry to Miss Forrest's bedsitter in Kensington, but each time she called the landlady was out, and no one else answered when she rang the bell. The other tenants must all be either deaf or totally absorbed in whatever they were doing to the exclusion of all other sounds, she decided. She had heard loud electronic music on one visit coming from somewhere overhead; it was so noisy that she was not surprised no one heard her ring. On her fourth attempt, however, she was successful. It was six o'clock in the evening, and the door was opened to her by a brassily blonde woman of about fifty wearing a purple caftan and many necklaces. Both the flowing robe and its wearer looked rather grubby; Miss Forrest was unlikely to have felt comfortable under the rule of such a châtelaine, Ellen thought, staring in surprise at the vision in the doorway, and what of Amelia on her visits? Though she had slept in a neighbouring hotel she must sometimes have come here.

She pulled herself together, for the woman was looking at her in an impatient manner.

"Well?" she asked, shifting her weight from one foot to the other and causing her necklaces to sway on her chest.

"Miss Mildred Forrest lived here?" asked Ellen, with some diffidence.

"That's right. Dead, though, she is. Had an accident, poor old thing," said the blonde, preparing to close the door.

"I know. She—she had a book of mine. Cicero's *Orations*, volume five of the Oxford edition," said Ellen. "I wonder if it's still here in her room?"

"Oh, one of them school books of hers, was it, dear? Well, sorry, you're too late. Gentleman's got it. Must have."

So David had got here before her. Why hadn't he let her know? But the landlady was still talking.

"Lady's brother, it was. Come from Surrey somewhere, after the funeral. He took all her things, not that there were many. I've let the room again now, to a nice young fellow. Plays in a group, he does. Don't want it standing idle, do I?"

Ellen supposed not.

"Just as well she didn't die here. Gives a place a bad name, people don't want the room after, not that it does to be choosy these days."

"Were there no letters? She hadn't left anything for anybody else?" Ellen asked.

"Not that I know of, dear, but then the gentleman would see to all that, I expect." Relenting a little, the blonde grew more forthcoming. "Kept herself to herself, she did, Miss Forrest. Been here years, I believe. Most of the tenants come and go, but she stayed on for ever, like the song says. I didn't know her well myself, but she had turned poorly-looking just lately. Can't say I was surprised, not really. Overdid it, at her age, all that studying."

"Studying?"

"Yes. That's what she was doing, wasn't it? Out all day, she was, at museums and things. 'Course, I only come here in July, I'm the manageress, but she'd gone off, I could see that," said the blonde. "Not like our other tenants, she wasn't."

Ellen could believe it.

"Still, better to go quick like she did than end up in one of them jerreetric wards, is what I say," added the landlady.

It would indeed have been terrible if Miss Forrest had ended in a geriatric ward, Ellen agreed. She walked away feeling profoundly depressed. What a set-up. The house, and doubtless many others in the area, must be owned by an absentee landlord who installed an overseer with plenty of time to pursue any individual sideline of their own. Poor Miss Forrest must have felt very much out of depth as the type of tenant changed. Soon the management would have found some way to get rid of her—she would have been forced out by increased rent, or even by the excuse of her age. Ellen had asked for the brother's address. The blonde had made a note of it, in case any bills came for Miss Forrest after her death, and reluctantly she invited Ellen in while she hunted for it among scraps of paper in a drawer of a shabby desk in what seemed to be her office. The whole house smelled, and the prevailing odours were not pleasant; Ellen, while she waited, detected boiling cabbage, cheap scent, musty damp, and an odd, smoky smell whose probable cause filled her with revulsion. Not the right sort of lodgings for Miss Forrest to have had at all, and no wonder she loved coming to Mulberry Cottage so much. She should still be there, Ellen thought, in sudden misery. Amelia should have left it to her for her lifetime.

Events were pressing in on her: thing's seemed to be hurtling on too fast for her to grasp their full significance. Isolated, like a tranquil island in the middle of it all, was the remembrance of her weekend in Oxford, a brief escape to sanity.

It was pointless to think of it again. She hurried away down the road, the damp leaves that littered the pavements eddying round her feet as she walked. David was staying up in town tonight and would be arriving at her flat in half an hour.

11

While Ellen was seeking the lost Cicero, Patrick, Jane and Michael were in Meldsmead. Michael had been eager to join the expedition and came home early from the office so that they might set out in good time. Patrick felt his brother-in-law did not quite trust him to look after Jane properly; but in fact Michael had become interested in the whole problem himself. He had been in America the first time Patrick had got mixed up with a sudden death that had turned out to be a murder; that time, Jane, unwillingly at first, had listened to his deductions and finally had helped tie in the ends. The next occasion had been when Patrick was in Austria; he had never told them the full details of what had happened, nor had any hint of his involvement been mentioned in the newspapers. He notices things that other people paid no heed to; and this time, Michael knew that Jane was worried because she thought Patrick was emotionally involved and in danger of losing his objectivity.

"You academic types are lucky, taking time off whenever you like. How often have you been down to this Hampshire hamlet in the past month?" Michael asked, as they set off. They were in his car, a sober grey Cortina; Patrick's white Rover had been seen often enough in Meldsmead.

"It's bigger than a hamlet. It's got a church and a pub and a garage," said Patrick, who was sitting in the back and hating it. He loathed being driven, but knew he must put up with it this time. "I've been there several times," he added airily. In fact he could have told them with accuracy the number of hours he had spent with

Ellen, apart from the details of his other visits to the village. "And I can't slope off whenever I want to. I work into the still hours, catching up, while you're sleeping peacefully in bed with my sister."

At any other time, Michael's retort to this would have been that Patrick should seek the embraces of a wife too, but now he tactfully refrained, in view of Jane's misgivings over Ellen.

"It soon won't be very peaceful, if Miss Conway is as active before she appears in this world as Andrew was," he said instead.

Jane's pregnancy still scarcely showed, but she had dressed this evening in a tunic over trousers, and a loose jacket, so that when she did her fainting act her condition should be unmistakeable. Patrick had been anxious in case she felt sensitive about being exploited in this state, but she reassured him. She was looking forward to meeting some of the people Patrick had described, and her one regret was that Ellen would not be there. Patrick said that on several Thursdays recently David Bruce had spent the night in London; it would be interesting to discover if he was doing so this week. As far as he could learn, Carol occasionally went off on writing assignments but more often stayed at home.

"What is the purpose of this expedition?" Michael asked as they headed southwards. They were approaching Meldsmead from a different direction than Patrick's usual route, since they had left from the Conway's house and not from Oxford, and they would enter the village from its other approach, the lane where Patrick had parked on his nocturnal exploration.

"We're hoping to meet lots of the locals," said Patrick. "I can't get the feel of the people involved in all this. I've met Carol Bruce once, and her husband twice. I don't know either of them as individuals, or Valerie Brinton. I've met her once, and seen her haring along in her car —she's a menace at the wheel."

"We won't see her tonight. She works in London, doesn't she?" said Jane.

"True—but we may be able to get the atmosphere of the place better than I've managed so far," Patrick said. "In Winterswick that time, you remember, I was staying with you, Jane, while Michael was away. It was easy to find excuses to visit the various people I was interested in. And in Austria it was the same; we were all cooped up in the mountains, cut off by an avalanche."

"You have been popping down to Meldsmead fairly often, Patrick. Michael's right."

"Yes, but it hasn't always been straightforward," Patrick said.

"It doesn't seem to me to be very much like Winterswick—the village, I mean—and it isn't like North Crowley either. Villages do seem to vary."

"North Crowley's going to end up a small town," Michael said, "but at the moment it's a pleasant place to live in."

"Meldsmead's much smaller," Patrick said. "And there hasn't been all that in-filling development. I should think several big landowners must own most of the surrounding country."

"Do you mean to say you don't know?" Michael asked mildly.

Patrick was suitably abashed.

"I haven't looked into it," he admitted.

"Maybe one of your illustrious colleges owns some of it," said Michael. "I've noticed that a number of rather unspoilt villages about the place belong to such institutions."

"Wouldn't you know, Patrick, if that was so about Meldsmead?" Jane asked.

"No. Only if it belonged to Mark's," said Patrick. "We do own quite a bit of property, but it's to the east of Oxford, mostly."

"It's agricultural, anyway, isn't it?" said Michael. "Meldsmead, I mean. So there wouldn't be a lot of building."

"I think the people who live there value their privacy too much to sell any plots nestling beside them for pure gain," said Patrick. "It's a prosperous area—people aren't going to jump onto the bandwagon of land speculation because they're affluent anyway."

"Lucky things," said Jane. "Well, I hope we achieve something. You'll probably find there's a British Legion meeting or something, and we can't burst in on anyone."

"I don't see how you'll discover anything if we do," said Michael. "I'm pretty embarrassed about the whole thing."

"You aren't at all. You're longing to do some detecting and pull Patrick down a peg," said Jane.

"We'll just have to play it by ear," Patrick said. "If we get in somewhere, and you two meet somebody, you can get talking—something may come up. For instance it may be common knowledge that, we'll say, Paul Newton —he's the pathologist—was given to going for walks beside the stream and wandering round Abbot's Lodge garden."

"He's melancholy, you said. He wouldn't devise accidents for Carol Bruce, though, would he?"

"Who can tell? Maybe he's unhinged," said Patrick. "No, I'm not looking for anything specific—just your reactions to the place, and another opportunity to see it for myself." He paused, then added, "We'll say we've been visiting friends and I've told you what a pleasant place Meldsmead is, hence our detour through the village."

"What friends, in case we have to give chapter and verse?" asked Michael.

"No need to be specific—evade an answer," Patrick said. "After all, Jane will be swooning. There'll be all that to divert whoever we meet."

Jane was feeling particularly well that evening. The lethargy she had experienced for some weeks past had gone; she felt alert and eager, not at all likely to buckle at the knees, but she hoped she would give an adequate dramatic performance.

It was almost dark when they reached the spot where Patrick had left the Rover before his two walks across the fields. He asked Michael to stop there so that he could point out to them the cross-country route to Abbot's Lodge. It was the sort of twilight when those out of doors can see quite well, but lights come on in houses and the sky, seen from within, seems navy blue. It was difficult to distinguish even the bulk of the house in the dusk, but Michael and Jane took Patrick's word for where it stood behind its hedge of yew. Then they drove on, and he pointed out the vicarage, the Queen Anne house which was the Kents' and the lanes leading to the Bradshaws' market garden and to Mulberry Cottage. They parked outside the Meldsmead Arms, and went into the saloon bar.

Patrick introduced Jane and Michael to Fred Brown and explained why they were in the village, in accordance with the plan they had made. It was early, and no one else was in the bar, which in a way was disappointing but it made his scheme for suggesting a stroll before they drove on easier to put into practice.

"Good job it's a fine night," said Jane, as they started up the road. "What would you have done if it had been raining?"

"Driven slowly, while we decided where to call," said Patrick.

They walked towards the centre of the village, Jane between them, arm-in-arm with both of them. She was too happy to worry about the rôle she was expected to perform soon, for she was with two of her favourite men; the third was safe at home with his excellent baby-sitter. It was a joy to her that Michael and Patrick got on so well together; though on the surface they seemed to be very different, in fact they were not so unlike each other. She could never have married a man who was dull or insensitive; and Patrick, though not particularly handy in the house because he had never had to do much cooking or carpentry was in fact very practical. Both of them were men who cared deeply about other people; Patrick considered indifference to be a cardinal sin, and often said so; Michael, without talking so much about his shared belief, practised it at work where his gift for smoothing ruffled feelings and the development of harmonious relations between departments was constantly exploited. Jane was so happy in her own marriage that she wished the same experience for her brother; but she knew no second best would do for him, and that was why nothing had come of various attachments in the past. Probably this Ellen was no better than anyone else he had been drawn to before; in fact, she must be less than admirable, or why did she prefer this David, a married man, to Patrick!

"Tell me when to faint," she said.

As she spoke they were nearing the turning to Mulberry Cottage, and the sound of a car could be heard from down the lane.

"Someone's coming," Michael said, superfluously.

They moved in to the side of the road; Patrick knew that the engine note was not that of Carol's Lancia. Sure enough, a mini paused for an instant at the junction into the main street and then turned right with a lurch before haring off towards the church.

"Valerie Brinton," Patrick said. What was she doing in the village in the middle of the week? She had been here before on a Thursday, he remembered, the night he had been so warmly welcomed by the Merrys. It must be some other house that they invaded tonight, he could not treat the kind vicar and his wife so summarily again.

"It was certainly a mini, but you couldn't be sure it was red, and you couldn't see the driver," Michael said.

"Correct. Always check your facts," said Patrick, cheerfully accepting the reproof.

"If we walk on a bit we may find out where she was going," Jane suggested.

"Sure you aren't tired?" asked Patrick.

"Not a bit. I'm enjoying it. Exercise is good for me. Tell him Michael."

"Exercise is good for her," Michael repeated obediently. "She's O.K. After all, when she does her faint, we can leave her and fetch the car. She needn't walk back."

"True."

They soon discovered where Valerie was going, for her car was parked outside the Kent's house.

"Don't they use their legs in this place?" Jane remarked. "It wouldn't have hurt her to walk."

"She must have been late," said Patrick. Was Valerie making a habit of using the cottage during the week? Perhaps she was exploring the possibilities of commuting to work.

"I think you'd better faint out here, Jane," he said. "In case you've forgotten, the Kents are the ones who are second time round in the marriage stakes—or he is. I haven't met her. Oh, by the way, keep quiet about having been at Slade House."

"This is the stockbroker?" Jane wanted to be sure of where they were going.

"That's right." Patrick was pleased to find she remembered what he had told her. "Oh, look," he went on, in lower tones. "Someone else is coming—with luck we may find it's a party. It's the pathologist, I think. Faint away, old girl."

Jane decided it was no use being embarrassed about gate-crashing a party. She uttered a small moan, came to a halt, and swayed realistically against Michael.

"What's the matter, darling? Are you feeling ill?" asked Michael, in such an affected voice that Jane nearly burst into giggles.

"I—I just feel a bit dizzy," she said, crossing her fingers to ward off ill-luck at the lie.

"Try putting your head down between your knees," Patrick advised.

"What's wrong? Someone not feeling well?" enquired a voice, and sure enough it was Paul Newton who now joined them on the path. He recognised Patrick and nodded to him, but curtly, his attention on Jane.

"It's all right—I just felt a bit giddy," she said. She was standing in such a way that her condition was unmistakeable; the roadway was illuminated by the porch light shining hospitably out from over the Kents' front door.

Meldsmead was much too small a village to have street lighting.

"Oh dear. You'd better sit down and rest. Come in here—this house belongs to friends of mine, and I'm just going to see them," said Paul. "And I happen to be a doctor." The final sentence was ground out of him. Patrick knew from medical friends the mixed emotions with which, in times of crisis, they thus revealed themselves.

"Come along," Paul said. "Can you manage her?"

He led the way up the short drive to the house, and Jane tottered behind, supported on either side by the other two. She made faint protesting sounds, to the effect that she was quite all right and not to bother, as they went. Patrick wondered if Paul Newton would be deceived by her act. They all trooped into the Kents' house, where Winifred Kent appeared in the hall wearing a welcoming smile which quickly changed to one of surprise as she saw three total strangers enter.

"Paul—?" she hesitated.

"Winnie, dear, good evening. I've just met someone strolling by who's feeling faint and knew you wouldn't mind your house being used for first aid," Paul said.

"Of course, Paul. Come in, my dear," said Winifred at once, in such a concerned voice that Jane felt very guilty. Michael and Patrick stepped back, and she was conducted, still wilting realistically, into an extremely elegant sitting-room where she was led to a large sofa. As Patrick had earlier suggested, she immediately put her head down on her knees. This was a wise action, for she did not look at all pale. Paul held her wrist, and after a few seconds said, "She'll be all right." Patrick hoped that stage fright had made her pulse erratic enough to convince the doctor that her near-faint was genuine.

There had been a babble of talk going on in the room when they all arrived, but naturally this had been halted by their sudden entrance. Brandy was proposed for the patient by Winifred, and approved by Paul. George Kent, who was hovering by the drinks trolley in a corner of the room, produced it, and Jane, who liked it, took a dainty sip.

"I'm quite all right now, really," she said. "I'm so sorry, what a silly thing to do. And you're having a party, oh, how awful."

She began to rise from among her cushions, but Winifred pushed her firmly back again.

"Wait a little longer, my dear, till you're quite better," she insisted. "This isn't a party—just a few friends, all quite informal."

"And we've met, haven't we?" George said to Patrick.

Patrick now made the necessary introductions and explanations. He glibly mentioned the mythical nearby friends, and Jane almost wished someone would cross-examine him to identify them, but no one did. Michael, good honest soul, was finding the acting part hard, but when a huge whisky was hospitably put into his hand and he had taken a swig he shed his inhibitions and began to praise the scenic beauty of the district with some verve.

"I'll go and get the car, and we'll push off," he said after a while. "Jane's all right now, aren't you, darling?"

"Yes, perfectly," said Jane, who looked blooming, spread out against the gold brocade upholstery of the sofa.

"No, no. You mustn't go yet. You must join the party," said Winifred.

The rest of the company had been talking together while all this had been going on. Patrick had seen that there were present only the Bradshaws, Valerie Brinton and Carol Bruce. At least, he supposed the woman with Denis Brandshaw was his wife.

She was. Winifred swiftly introduced everybody.

"We knew Valerie was here for the night, and she told us that Carol's a grass widow for the evening," Winifred said. "I used to be a real widow myself, and I know how lonely it can be, so we thought we'd get together here, and Paul too of course." Her gaze flitted from Paul to Valerie. Patrick, intently watching though he stood looking particularly vague, followed the drift of her thoughts instantly. She was obviously happy in her new marriage. Had she, a lonely widow, come between George and his first wife? She was about forty, plump as he had earlier been told, but still attractive, with a real warmth to her. Madge Bradshaw, the only other person in the room whom he had not met before, was much the same age; she wore a jersey suit and had very good legs and small smartly-shod feet. She was taller than Denis, who seemed subdued compared with how genial he had been in the pub when Patrick had met him before.

"It's Winifred's birthday," Denis said. "Many happies, my dear." He raised his glass, and now that everyone felt the invalid was on the mend the party began. Jane, on her sofa, was at the disadvantage of any seated guest, but as soon as Winifred had prettily accepted the greetings of the company she perched on the end of the sofa and began to ask her uninhibitedly about the forthcoming baby.

Patrick joined George, who was talking to Valerie and Carol, while Michael discussed gardening with the Bradshaws. Valerie wore a lime-green trouser suit and huge dangling earrings; she was easily the smartest woman in the room. Carol was dressed in some soft woollen material in pale fawn; she looked rather more fragile than he remembered.

It would have been odd not to have spoken to Valerie about Mulberry Cottage, Ellen and Miss Forrest, and Patrick did so, in that order.

"I was sorry about Miss Forrest," he said.

"Yes, it was shocking," Valerie agreed. "Of course, there was nothing of her. A puff of wind would have blown her away. Her heart was very dicky, and she'd been very upset by my aunt's death."

Patrick had a sudden mental picture of Miss Forrest collapsing into a little bundle on the stairs in the British Museum. But she hadn't just folded up; she'd rolled down the whole of the first flight, with impetus, then lain spread-eagled on the middle landing. Would she really have pitched down so far from just a heart attack?

He supposed so: it was probably a question of weight distribution, however minute the body. Miss Brinton, too, had pitched down the steps of the Acropolis.

"Did you meet Miss Forrest?" he asked Carol. "She was your neighbour, wasn't she?"

"No, we never met," said Carol. "She left just as we moved in. It was a tragic thing to happen to her."

"You've been very kind about the books, Dr. Grant," Valerie said. "Ellen has kept me posted with your various dealings. I'm gratified to find they're worth something. I was afraid they'd be to obscure. Superseded by more modern translations."

"Oh no. The classic editions are always in demand," Patrick said. "It's just a question of finding the person who really wants each one."

"Well, you've taken a lot of trouble and I'm grateful," Valerie said.

"I wonder if that volume of Cicero's *Orations* has turned up yet," Patrick said.

"Oh? What was that?" asked Valerie.

"There's an Oxford edition of the *Letters* and the *Orations*," Patrick said. "Miss Forrest had listed both as being complete, but volume five of the *Orations* was missing. Neither Ellen nor I could find it. We thought it must have been replaced in a different shelf."

"That's unlike Milly. She was methodical," Valerie said. "I expect it will turn up."

"It spoils the set, does it, to have a volume missing?" Carol asked.

"Well, it's a standard text always in print, so it could be replaced," Patrick said. "And the whole set's not of great value—it would just save an impecunious student having to buy it at the full cost of a new one."

"I see," said Carol.

"How are you settling down now?" Patrick asked her. "I suppose you've got workmen all over the place?"

"We haven't finished deciding what's to be done," she said. "I think you need to live in a house for a time before you can be certain how you want things."

"Very true," said Madge Bradshaw. "We made lots of mistakes through trying to get everything done at once. We'd lived in quarters much of the time in our Army life, and I suppose we just lacked experience. But you see so many houses in your work, don't you, Carol? That must give you plenty of ideas."

"Yes—it's a question of trying to include all the best ones," Carol said.

"What is your work?" Patrick asked. There was no reason for her to suppose that he knew; and what he had heard had been very vague: some sort of free-lance journalism.

"I write about houses where interesting people live, and about interesting people—women in unusual jobs, that sort of thing," Carol said. "I'd like to do a piece about this house, it's so lovely. But I'm not sure if I'll be able to."

"She means because we aren't particularly interesting as inhabitants," said George. "Anyway, it's not a museum piece. You should see it when my daughters are at home. One's at the university and one's working in London. When they're home there's coffee on the carpets and records blaring away."

"And we love it," Winifred said, patting him as she joined their group. "I haven't any children of my own. It's lovely to have a ready-made family."

"These two are rather sweet," said Valerie. "They believe in happy-ever-after."

"Yes, we do," said Winifred. "Now come and talk to Paul." She led Valerie firmly off, watched by Carol and Patrick with some amusement.

"Winifred's determined to pull that one off. Because she's been lucky second time round she want's everyone else to be paired off neatly. Paul's a widower," Carol said.

"I'd heard that," Patrick said. "Won't it work?" He watched Paul and Valerie; they were talking together in a friendly way.

"Things never do if you set them up," said Carol.

"They have to be spontaneous." Her tone was ironic. Patrick tried to conceal how interested he was in observing her; this was the woman whose husband was having an affair with Ellen. What was wrong in her marriage that made her cynical and made her husband stray? He hoped Jane, from her sofa, was able to cast a few shrewd glances in this direction and make some assessment. As far as he could tell, Carol seemed attractive; she was well made-up but not aggressively, and her dress looked expensive. She was obviously competent: too competent, perhaps. It was very easy to understand how David found Ellen so much more appealing, for so did he. He's too old for Ellen, thought Patrick crossly.

"I was sorry about your dog," he said.

"Oh yes. It was sad. I'd forgotten, of course it was you who found poor Rufus. David told me. Clever of you to know whose dog it was."

Patrick opened his mouth to say that Ellen knew; then he realised that David must have suppressed her part in the incident. Denis had not included her in his account of it.

"I'd seen the dog when I met you that first time, before you moved in," he reminded her, keeping his head.

Michael had been talking to the Bradshaws for a while, his reactions to them could be discovered later. Patrick felt that not much more could be usefully learnt by staying any longer and he did not want to strain the Kent's good-will too far.

"Jane, if you're all right, shall I go and get the car? We've trespassed quite long enough on our hosts' kindness," he said.

"I'm fine," said Jane, and stood up, with a glance at Paul, who still stood beside Valerie obediently exchanging small talk with her, like a good guest, but not looking very animated.

A small tussle of looks now took place between Michael and Patrick about the car, but Patrick held Michael's gaze sternly.

"Oh—will you fetch it? Thanks," Michael said, finally giving in.

"You'd better stay with Jane. I won't be long," said Patrick.

Michael gave him the keys, and Patrick left the house. Once out in the road he broke into a brisk trot. He was very fit, because he took a boat out on the river at least twice a week. He loped off down the lane that led to Mulberry Cottage, sped past, and went on to Abbot's Lodge. As he had hoped, the back door was unlocked. He went in, using his small flat pocket torch, and made his way to the drawing-room. He looked round quickly, shining the light on bookshelves stacked with expensive books full of coloured plates, coffee table books, he'd heard them called, and then on a beautiful Sheraton bureau.

He was only in the room three minutes but he found something that interested him very much. Then he ran back up the lane and fetched the car.

"What a long time you were," said Michael, earning several black marks.

"I—er—we'd left the car at the pub—I popped in—er —" Patrick searched about for a suitable phrase for mixed company.

Jane rescued him.

"Oh, please, before you go, may I do the same?" she pleaded looking suddenly pitiful, and Winifred bore her aloft to the bathroom.

III

"I'll buy you dinner on the way home," Patrick said, as they drove away down the lane.

"It's the least you can do. What an embarrassing hour," said Michael. "I hope you got what you wanted. They all seemed thoroughly nice, ordinary types to me."

"I didn't think they were at all ordinary," said Jane. "I was fascinated."

"Where are we going to eat?" Michael interrupted. "I'm starving, I only had a sandwich for lunch so as to leave the office early."

"Poor old you," said Jane. "Patrick and I had genteel afternoon tea with Andrew, didn't we, Patrick? Toast and honey."

"There's a good pub about seven miles on," said Patrick. He'd marked it as another spot to take Ellen if he got the chance. "Let's go there—turn right at the next crossroads. It's not really out of our way."

"Nice house your new chums have got," Jane said. They must be doing all right."

"You were hours upstairs with Winifred," said Michael.

"She showed me around, and I sat on her bed nattering," said Jane. "I wasn't wasting time."

"You were probably admiring the interior decorating scheme," said Michael. "I bet it's lavish. Stockbrokers always have to give the impression of affluence, even if they're on the bread-line. He's probably shelling out alimony to wife number one, and living on tick."

"You are horrible, darling," said Jane. "I don't think it's like that at all. I think wife number one died or skipped off. The daughters clearly live with their father when they're at home."

At this point they reached the Horse and Jockey, where they were to eat, and the discussion was halted while Patrick arranged for a table. The pub was not busy, so they went straight into the restaurant and ordered their meal.

Over the avocados, Jane said: "Winifred was sweet—so kind. I'd be furious if three strangers gate-crashed my party."

"You wouldn't, dear. You'd be another ministering angel, just as she was," said Michael.

"Well, up to a point, needs must, I suppose," said Jane. "Rise to the occasion, I mean. It would be a good dodge for burglars, wouldn't it—while everyone is tending the sickly person, an accomplice is upstairs looting the place."

"You are quite like your brother after all, aren't you? Given to wild imaginings," Michael said, grinning.

"Winifred was wasting her time with that matchmaking ploy, anyway," said Patrick. "Newton just wasn't interested. But I can see why Winifred thought of it—Valerie must be the right sort of age, and she's no pinhead—she'd be a match for him intellectually. Romance isn't everything."

"Would you fancy her?" Jane asked.

"You're always asking me that sort of question," said Patrick. "But the answer is no, I wouldn't."

"She's older than you," Jane said. "Is that the reason?"

"No, not at all. It isn't anything to do with that. Age needn't come into it at all—it just depends on the individual people. But there's something formidable about Valerie."

"What do you think, Mike?" Jane pursued. "You know I'm always anxious to find out who appeals to you, so that I can watch out for danger."

"Idiot," said Michael, laughing at her. "But I agree with Patrick—I didn't find her attractive, and it's not an age thing. She's smart, and intelligent, and animated."

"Frightens you both, maybe," said Jane. "You prefer cosier types."

"I certainly prefer cuddlier ones," said Michael. "She's a bit angular."

"Did you see how she lit up when Carol and she were talking?" said Jane. "I've never seen that spark between two women before."

The two men looked at her. There was a silence.

"Are you sure about that?" Patrick asked.

"I'm sure there was a spark between them. I won't go further than that," Jane said sedately.

"They like each other?" Patrick said. "Why not?"

"Come off it, Patrick. Jane thinks Valerie's gay," said Michael. "Don't you, darling?"

"I do deplore the way English usage has declined," said Patrick in dour tones. "Adjectives used in total innocence can have quite another meaning. But are you sure of this, Jane?"

"No, of course not. It's a subject I know nothing about, except in theory," Jane replied. "But she had the sort of look on her face that you see when a woman is attracted to a man. You often notice it at parties—you know what I mean."

"And Carol?" Patrick asked. "How did she react?"

"I couldn't see her face so well. She seemed quite happy. For heaven's sake don't go leaping to conclusions, Patrick. I expect it's slanderous even to think of it."

"Can't women spot this among themselves?" Patrick demanded. "Men can, soon enough."

"No. I can't, anyway. I never think about it," Jane said. "Sometimes, of course, if it's very blatant, then one does. But nowadays people always leap to the worst conclusions if two women live together just for company, or because it's cheaper. Why can't they just be friends. That's what they are."

"Why not, indeed," said Michael mildly.

"People think everyone gets a chance to marry if they want to—they don't," Jane said, becoming keen to make her point. "Not if they're particular, that is. And there are plenty of people—men and women—who just aren't interested in sex. That doesn't mean they're queer though they get talked about as if they must be."

"No, poor things, they're just missing lots of fun," said Michael, who liked to see Jane grow enthusiastic as she talked.

"You don't have to convince me, Jane. I know you're right," said Patrick.

"Thank goodness you've always had a series of girl-friends, Patrick, otherwise goodness knows what would be said about you," Jane told him.

Patrick laughed.

"Thanks very much," he said. "I hope one glance is enough for anyone to know what I am. But let's get back to Valerie. She's a tough customer, but then she's a very successful career woman. She may be one of these disinterested types, or she may never have felt strongly enough for any man to want to give up her job and darn his socks instead."

"Figuratively speaking, you mean," said Jane. "Women can stick to their careers if they want to. Carol has."

"I wonder why the Bruces haven't any children," Patrick mused.

"Probably some awful tragedy," Jane said promptly. "Winifred had one that died, by her first husband. She told me so, upstairs. She said it was awful later. People used to make snide remarks about 'of course, you haven't any children so you can do this and that—' when they'd have loved a family."

By now they were eating veal cooked in madeira, and drinking claret. "What else did you talk about, while you were closeted upstairs?" Patrick asked his sister. "Have the Kents been married long?"

"No. Only a few months," said Jane. "And where do you think they went for their honeymoon?" She waited. "To Greece," she said.

"I can think of no more perfect place," said Patrick instantly.

"Winifred never met Amelia," Jane said. "I said how you'd come to the village originally because of being literally in at her death. And she said how awful it had been—the accident—and how she'd been looking forward to seeing her again."

"But you said they'd never met?"

"No—I mean they never met since Winifred came to Meldsmead. She was at Slade House."

Patrick stared.

"Winifred was at Slade House?" Michael wanted to get it quite clear.

"Yes. Long before my day, of course. And if Amelia heard that George was going to marry again, she'd have heard Winifred spoken of by her former married name, and wouldn't connect it. Anyway, I don't suppose the old girl and George were buddies, exactly—not much in common."

"So she must have known Miss Forrest too."

"Of course. I didn't find out if they'd met while Miss Forrest was in Meldsmead—sorry about that, Patrick, but I was too busy concentrating on not saying I'd been at Slade House too."

"I'm glad you kept that quiet," said Patrick.

"You told me to," said Jane. "By the way, I got Miss Chesterfield's address—you asked me for it. She's still in Africa."

"Oh. What a great pity."

Michael had to be told about Miss Chesterfield and the photograph album.

"Winifred might be in it. She'd know some of the names, perhaps," said Jane.

Patrick suddenly stood up.

"Excuse me," he said abruptly. "I've got to make a phone call."

Jane watched him go with astonishment.

"Has he suddenly gone coy? Dons are sometimes more inhibited than other men, but not in front of their kith and kin, surely? Or do you think he really meant it? Is he going to ring Ellen up?"

"I should imagine he meant what he said," Michael answered. "Maybe he promised to call her at a certain hour."

"He wouldn't have forgotten, then. He'd have been looking at his watch all the evening. He changed suddenly when I told him Winifred had been at Slade House."

"I can't see why this business is needling him so," Michael said. "Life is full of strange events, after all, and weird coincidences."

"Poor old Patrick. I'm afraid that Ellen's sent him rather off balance," Jane said. "She must be a bit dumb, don't you think? Surely he's quite a dish? One can't tell, of course, about one's own brother, but girls are always after him."

"He's usually got some bird or other around," Michael agreed. "And he's eligible to a degree."

"Wary, though, now," said Jane. "Too wary. Suddenly he'll find all the best girls have been snapped up."

"I think he's found it quite easy up till now to have fun without getting hurt himself," Michael said. "This girl's playing hard to get."

"It's not that. She's besotted with this David person," Jane said. "Girls are so silly. They get some wretched man into their system, and however doomed the whole thing is, they don't seem able to cure themselves. How nice to be married and out of the war."

For some people the war only began after marriage, Michael reflected. But he and Jane were among the lucky ones. He leaned across the table and kissed her nose, and Patrick witnessed this touching incident as he returned to his seat.

"Was she there?" Jane asked.

"I wasn't ringing Ellen," Patrick said. "That blackberry and apple pie I took from Carol's dust-bin—I didn't tell you before—there were a few laburnum seeds in it. Not many—not enough to be lethal, unless one person ate them all. We don't know, of course, how many were in the bit Carol ate. I was ringing Colin up."

"Colin? Why suddenly, tonight?"

"I'm going to see him at New Scotland Yard tomorrow. I should have gone before, but there was nothing concrete to tell him. There still isn't, really. But he can make a few enquiries," Patrick said.

"I should have thought laburnum seeds in the pie were definite evidence," Michael said grimly.

"That's why you asked me if Michael ever made pastry," Jane said slowly.

"What?" Michael exclaimed.

"I'll explain later, darling," Jane told him.

"I certainly don't," said Michael.

Patrick had suddenly become very quiet and depressed; no wonder, Jane thought, if he suspected David Bruce of putting laburnum seeds in Carol's pie.

"David didn't eat any of that pie, you see," Patrick said. "When Carol was ill, it was there, in the fridge, but he had none. Naturally he wouldn't eat it, if he knew it would be poisonous."

"What about the dog? Did it eat something meant for Carol? Is that what you think?" Jane demanded.

"It must be what happened," Patrick said. "Look, eat up, you two. Do you mind? I think I'd like to get back. I'll have to cancel some pupils tomorrow."

"All right. I'm full, anyway," said Jane. "It was a lovely dinner, Patrick."

He made an effort. "We'll have another one when all this is finished," he said. "And dally with the port."

Jane did not dare to say she hoped that Ellen would be with him.

IV

Fortunately Patrick had no lecture the following day. One of his pupils was due for a tutorial at ten; luckily the young man lived in college and straight after breakfast Patrick went round to see him, reversing the more usual process by himself being the one to postpone their appointment. The pupil, roused tousle-headed and unshaven by his knock, was mightily relieved in fact since he had set his alarm early in the hope that he might manage to finish the essay Patrick should have heard.

After this Patrick got into the car and went to London for his appointment with Detective-Inspector Colin Smithers. They had met when Colin was a sergeant assisting in an enquiry at Winterswick; with promotion he had transferred to the Metropolitan Police.

Colin kept him waiting, but not for long. He was a red-headed, freckle-faced man with a deceptively ingenuous air; imaginative, as well as tenacious.

"I've got someone delving about at Somerset House—they haven't come up with anything yet," Colin greeted him. "Have you any more to tell me?"

"Here's the analyst's report on that pie. He was slow producing it—he's a friend of mine, and he happened to be away when I sent it round to his rooms, so it grew a bit mouldy. But the laburnum was in it."

Colin glanced at the report.

"You didn't get in touch with me before," he pointed out. "Except to ask about that post-mortem on the old lady who died in the British Museum."

"I'd nothing to go on," Patrick said. "No evidence."

"This is evidence all right," Colin said, tapping the report.

"I brought it in case you thought I'd made it up," said Patrick.

"Any hunch you have is worth acting on—why don't you give up Oxford and join us? I'm sure you could have special promotion for late entry," said Colin with a grin.

"I have my uses as a civilian infiltrator," Patrick said. "Are you going to dig up the dog?"

"Not immediately, no. We've no crime, you see. It's tricky."

"Agreed. We've got to prevent one," Patrick said.

"The dog could easily have eaten something meant for Carol Bruce—something she didn't fancy. Barbiturates, perhaps, since laburnum seeds usually lead to vomiting, before coma. The fact that he collapsed into the river might be sheer chance—he staggered about and fell there."

"But it can't be David Bruce. Why should he want to kill his wife?" Patrick said.

"Why would anyone else want to?" Colin asked. "Most murders are committed by spouses, you know."

"Cold-bloodedly pre-meditated ones?" asked Patrick. "Have you found out any more about Miss Forrest?"

"I've got a man calling on the brother this morning," Colin said. "He'll go through her effects—if they haven't been disposed of by now, that is. Don't be too hopeful."

"He'll remember the Cicero, anyway, if it was there," Patrick said. "It must be somewhere, after all. It might throw some light on all this, though I can't think how." What significant marginal notes could there possibly be in the volume?

"Then there's Ellen Brinton. Now how do you think she fits into this business?" Colin leaned back in his chair and surveyed Patrick across his desk. "You've only her word for it that she'd arranged to meet Miss Forrest that day."

"She's just an innocent bystander who's unfortunately involved," said Patrick shortly. "And how's little Cathy?"

Colin blushed to the roots of his carroty hair.

"Oh, very well," he mumbled.

It was Colin's visit to see Cathy Ludlow while she was up at Oxford that had caused him and Patrick to renew their acquaintance. Catherine had come down that summer with a respectable second.

"What's she doing now? Working in London?"

"She's in Paris. But she'll be home for Christmas."

"Well, Paris isn't far away. I expect you've kept in touch," Patrick remarked.

"She must see the world a bit," Colin said. "She's still pretty young."

"Don't risk losing her, though," Patrick said, suddenly serious. "A second chance doesn't always come one's way."

"No. I'll remember that," Colin said, looking embarrassed.

Patrick had not revealed to Colin that he had any particular interest in Ellen; she was just a character in a puzzling drama that he felt certain was unfolding. He had told Colin that he suspected David Bruce of having an affair outside his marriage, but he had not said with whom; however, if they watched David Bruce, as now they might after the discovery of the pie, the police would very soon find out. His heart felt heavy, but she had to be extracted somehow from this mire.

"If we had the pie, and not your amateur chum, and if we'd had a tidy slice of it, we'd have been able to find out if it was home-made, or made of frozen pastry, or sold ready-made," Colin said.

"Do I detect a reproof?" Patrick asked. "I stole it anyway, from the Bruces' dustbin. Whoever put it there might have decided to pluck it back and burn it, and if much had gone, could have noticed someone had had a go at it."

"That's true. Perhaps you did right," Colin said. "But do be careful, Patrick. You'll be breaking and entering next."

"I've done that too," said Patrick, with calm. "At least, I didn't have to break, either time, but I've entered. And I wasn't caught." He described his visit to the shed at

Mulberry Cottage and his theft of the photograph album, and last night's quick visit to Abbot's Lodge.

Colin listened without interrupting.

"That's very interesting, but it's not enough for us to act on," he said at last. "And we can't use this analysis as an excuse. If someone means to get Carol, they'll do it. It sounds to me as if they're just trying to scare her off—small accidents about the place—the death of the dog. An ill-wisher could have slipped out of the Bradshaws' party and let down the tyre of her car. Someone wants her to go. Maybe David wants her to leave him. He'd have his weekends in peace with Ellen then, wouldn't he? You say she uses the cottage."

"I never told you—" Patrick began to protest.

"No, but I get hunches too," Colin said, and as he spoke the telephone rang.

He answered it, listened, and covering the mouthpiece with his hand said to Patrick, "It's Surrey."

Patrick sat there while Colin said: "Yes, I see. No, don't do any more yet, thanks," and rang off. He then made a great business of putting away his biro and straightening the papers in front of him.

"Well, come on. What's happened?" Patrick demanded.

"We've been forestalled," Colin said. "A young woman collected a volume of Cicero early this morning. A Miss Ellen Brinton."

After he left Colin, Patrick went to the British Museum, where he stood looking at the caryatid again and wishing she were placed somewhere with a comfortable chair in front of her instead of in a cramped space filled by a column. Then he had a ham roll and some coffee in the refreshment room and after that he soothed himself by contemplating some illuminated manuscripts. Then, by arrangement, he returned to New Scotland Yard to see if Colin had found out anything else; his researcher at Somerset House must, by now, have unearthed some dates, if nothing else. Colin was out, so once again he had to wait. He always carried some small volume or other in his pocket to while away any idle hours he might meet with, and was immersed in the work of an obscure modern poet when Colin at last appeared.

"Sorry, Patrick. Have you been waiting long?" Colin hung up his raincoat, gave a few commands to the sergeant who had followed him into his office, and then turned to his visitor.

"Not really. You've found something?" Patrick said.

"Yes. Some details about David Bruce." Colin told him what they were.

Patrick drove home by way of Ellen's flat. She was out, and though he waited for some time she did not return. It was Friday. She must have left London for the weekend. Perhaps she had never come back after her visit to Surrey.

He gave up. By the time he got back to Oxford it was much too late to dine, so he scrambled himself some eggs which he ate while listening to Bach on his record player. At ten o'clock, Jane rang up.

"I've been looking through that Old Slade House photograph album you stole," she said. "I've recognised someone. I think you'd better come over."

"I'll be there in half-an-hour," said Patrick.

PART EIGHT

I

Jane was in her dressing-gown sitting on the floor by the fire. She had washed her hair, and it hung on her shoulders, soft and silky. Her face was filled out a little and she looked serene. However, when Patrick came in, bringing with him an aura of the crisp, frosty night, her expression was alert enough.

"Michael's out at a village meeting. He won't be long," she said. "I was just browsing through the album while I dried my hair. Here." She handed it to him.

Patrick, still wearing his overcoat, sat down facing her.

"I've put a marker in the page," she said.

Patrick opened the volume at the place indicated. There were groups of girls in gym tunics, and several of girls in costume, dressed for a performance of *She Stoops to Conquer*, according to the legend below. Patrick studied them all carefully.

"Ah! Here!" he exclaimed, his finger on the image of one girl.

"That's right," Jane looked at him. "It's the hair that's so different," she said. "I was amusing myself going through the album trying to imagine them all much older now, and with different hair. I suddenly saw it."

"You knew who you were looking for," Patrick said.

"No, I didn't," Jane protested. "Nor did you, or you'd

have said so and we'd have looked through the album accordingly."

"I've been looking for the link with Slade House all the time, and now you've found it," Patrick said.

"Winifred Kent made no secret of having been at Slade House," Jane said.

Patrick looked at the photograph of a slim girl dressed as a man in regency style, and wearing a full-bottomed wig.

"She told you when you were alone upstairs?" Patrick asked. "No one else heard?"

"No," Jane said.

"After we'd gone, they may have talked about us. Valerie had mentioned the books. It's no secret that I was in Athens when Miss Amelia died," Patrick said. "I wonder if she said it again." He took a penknife from his pocket and very gently prised the edges of the photograph away from its mount. It came free quite easily, pasted in only at the corners. In faded ink on the back were written the names of the girls. He handed it silently to Jane.

"We should have thought of looking on the backs," he said.

"But with the married name—we wouldn't have realised," Jane said.

"We could have checked them all," Patrick said.

"But now we know this, does it make any difference?" Jane asked.

"Indeed it does," said Patrick.

"I don't see why. The two who might have recognised her are dead."

"And why are they dead? Because she didn't want to be recognised," said Patrick.

"You mean Miss Forrest was somehow pushed down those stairs? You've always thought that, haven't you?"

"I mean Miss Forrest was pushed and also Miss Amelia. That youth who jostled her did it on purpose."

"But how? Who? A hired yobo?"

"No. It was much more subtle," said Patrick. "But I

don't know if I can prove it." He looked at Jane. "You said that Miss Amelia wouldn't forgive a past pupil who trespassed against her code. If she met such a pupil in later life she might feel it her duty to expose to anyone closely involved the past misdeeds of that girl."

"If she'd made a new life—a good marriage—" Jane's voice trailed off. "Would she be so cruel?"

"We can't know. She might watch and wait. But the girl—woman—would never feel safe."

He stood up.

"I've got to get down there, Jane. Someone else may be in terrible danger."

"What, now? In the middle of the night?"

"Yes." In his mind was the thought of Ellen; she had collected the missing *Cicero* that day. Why had it been missing? Would someone else be after it too?

"I'd better ring Colin before I go—that is, if I can find him," he said, but as he finished speaking the telephone rang.

Jane rose somewhat ponderously to her feet and went out to the hall to answer it. She was back in less than a minute.

"Telepathy," she said. "It's Colin for you. He tried Mark's, and when you weren't there, thought of us."

But Patrick had not waited to hear her sentence end. She heard him say, "Oh God," to something Colin said, and then, "What happened?" There was silence for a few moments while Colin spoke, and then Patrick told him about the photograph. After that a few more remarks were exchanged and Patrick came back into the sitting-room.

"What is it?" Jane scarcely dared to ask.

"It's Madge Bradshaw. She's been killed," he said. "Her body was found in the church this afternoon. It seems something was dropped on her head from above."

"Oh no!"

"The church has got a spy-hole in the belfry so that the bell-ringers can see when to start ringing the wedding peal. Our villain was waiting for her up there and dropped a great stone on her as she passed below. And in case she'd only been stunned, she'd been cracked a few times on the skull with a huge brass candlestick."

"But why was she in the church at all?"

"She helped a lot with church affairs, remember? She'd been cleaning some of the brass—taken bits home to clean, it seems, and was returning it. I'm going over there, Jane."

"But it's happened—it's awful—but surely—?" Jane stopped talking as she saw his stricken face.

"Colin heard about this because he'd got on to the local police down there and asked to be told if anything unusual came in about Meldsmead or that area. The local C.I.D. have been pretty efficient. They say the body lay face downwards on the floor of the church and the head had been smashed in."

"But it's—it's maniacal," Jane said.

"Yes," Patrick agreed. "I'm afraid we're dealing with a maniac, and it's become a desperate situation."

"Can't the police—?" Jane looked at him fearfully.

"They've done all their stuff so far—carted off the body, made enquiries in the village, closed the church up till tomorrow. Colin's going down there right away to tell them what we know. It's not a Yard matter yet, but I suppose it may become one. We've got to have proof, you see and here's a part of it." He put the photograph carefully in his wallet. "I'm off now, Jane. I'll be in touch."

She heard his car racing up through the gears as he tore out of the village without any regard for the speed limit, and she knew there was no way at all for her to help him.

II

Patrick's car burnt up the miles to Meldsmead. It was another fine, dry night; a fresh breeze was blowing, keeping the clouds away, and the sky was studded with stars. Driving conditions were good and there was little traffic once he left the main roads behind. He tried to calm himself by reasoning that the murderer was most unlikely to strike again that night; the plans had all been laid long ago, the despatch of Miss Amelia carefully arranged. But Miss Forrest had been killed, he was sure, on some impulse; and now Madge Bradshaw's death had shown a loss of nerve.

Colin was going down to Meldsmead with the knowledge and consent of his chief; unless the Yard was called in, the investigation would be dealt with by the local force, and tactful co-operation would be needed. He had assured Patrick on the telephone that it was impossible for anything more to happen during the hours of darkness, but Patrick did not share this view. Something had been overlooked; someone was in danger; and swifter action might have saved Madge. Colin had promised to come and find him in the village as soon as he had finished with the local Superintendent.

"I'll know where to look for you," he'd added grimly.

Patrick approached the village from the north-east, the direction he had taken with Jane and Michael only the evening before. He drove fast along the lanes, trusting to be warned by the headlights of any approaching car. As long as it's not our Valerie, he thought; but she would be back by now, if she was spending tonight in the village. She'd said at the Kent's house the night before that she was going to the office as usual today.

He paused at the turning where the lane joined the main village street; the church lay on the left. Everything seemed quiet. Patrick pulled the car round so the headlights illuminated the little green in front of the church; beside it was the graveyard. There seemed to be no police guard. He got out of the car and walked up to the church gate. A big padlock and chain secured it; he supposed the door into the church itself would be locked too. He turned back towards the car, sniffing: there was the smell of an autumn bonfire in the air; someone had been burning their garden rubbish. Suddenly Patrick knew that this was no ordinary bonfire. He leaped back into the car and accelerated up the lane, past the darkened houses. No one seemed to be about. He supposed the police had made enquiries about Madge's last known movements at every house. The body had been found by the vicar at four o'clock.

He turned into the lane leading to Abbot's Lodge and drove down it as fast as he dared; then he stopped outside Mulberry Cottage, automatically switching off his headlights. At first glance everything seemed normal as he opened the gate and strode up the path. He saw at once that the curtains were drawn across the windows, unlike the night when he had found the photograph album. Someone was inside, and it was not Valerie, for there was no sign of her car.

The smell of smoke was much stronger here. He looked up at the roof, but it seemed to be all right. Then he walked round to the westerly side of the cottage and what he saw there made his heart plummet. The thick eaves above his head were glowing red, like an inferno, fanned by the prevailing wind towards the rear of the cottage, and as he ran round he could see clouds of smoke billowing out of the thatch. Even as he stood there, horrified, tongues of flame began to dart through the weight of old straw.

"Ellen!" he shouted, frantically, first under the windows where he stood, and then at the front of the cottage; but there was no answer from within.

The back door had panels of glass in its upper half; he was wearing gloves, and with his fist he smashed a hole in the pane nearest the door handle, reached in, and turned the key. The door did not yield. Careful Ellen had bolted it. But Patrick was heavy and with his shoulder to the frame he soon broke it open. As it burst inwards and he entered the building he feared the draught might cause a funnel of air to sweep through the house and fan the flames, but there was no sign of any fire in the kitchen. He opened its further door, which led into the living-room, very cautiously. There was a strong smell of smoke here. He knew there were two bedrooms above. Ellen must have been overcome by the fumes as she lay asleep. He blundered his way up the stairs, groping in the dark, for his torch was in the car, and opened the first door he found, still calling her name.

She was in the room, and did not stir as he snatched her up out of the bed and stumbled back down the stairs again, carrying her. He took her out into the garden, removed his own overcoat and wrapped her in it; she wore only a thin nightdress. Then he gave her a little shake, and she moaned slightly.

"David," she mumbled.

"Ellen, wake up! You're all right, Ellen," he told her, but she seemed able only to moan. Fresh air was the best thing for her, and she could come to no more harm for a few minutes while he got help to deal with the fire. So far it seemed confined to the roof, and there was just a chance that the telephone might still be working. He laid her on the ground, near the fence in front of the cottage, well away from all flying sparks which would blow in the other direction, and went back into the house by way of the kitchen again.

The telephone, he remembered, was on the window-sill in the living-room above a book-shelf. Arms outstretched, feeling for the furniture standing in his way, he managed to get across the room without more damage than a bruised shin. By some miracle the line was intact, and he dialled 999. Then he moved to the front door, which was close beside him. It was not bolted, merely closed on the yale lock, and the chain was not pulled across. How strange of Ellen to have bolted the back door so carefully and not this one; perhaps she had confidence in its solid oak. As he opened it and pulled it inwards the door caught against something that lay on the floor, preventing it from opening fully. Patrick's foot brushed against something. He bent down. A solid object lay there; he felt cloth, then hair. It was a human body. Someone else was there in the room.

Patrick dragged the body through the doorway into the garden, and Colin arrived just in time to help him.

"My God," he said. "You were right."

"Yes," said Patrick. "But I didn't think of arson. Ellen's over by the fence. She seems very dopey, as if she's been drugged. Perhaps it's just the smoke."

"This one's alive. The pulse is quite strong," Colin said. "Who is it?"

Grimly, Patrick told him.

"The fire brigade's coming, but I didn't call an ambulance," he added. "Why on earth aren't there any coppers down at the church?"

"Calm down, Patrick. There's no blaze showing here yet, they wouldn't have seen it if there had been," Colin said.

"I smelled it," Patrick told him. "They could have done that."

But Colin was looking down at the victims of the fire.

"This must have been planned," he said, thinking aloud. "They've both been doped. They'd be coughing and spluttering if the fire had made them unconscious. Look, they're both stirring. Another half-hour or so and they'd have suffocated. This place will go up like a match-box soon."

"Christ, what a devil," said Patrick.

"We'll get them away," Colin decided. "Quick, before anyone else arrives here. Our villain will think the scheme worked. It's most unlikely anyone else in the village knew that Ellen was here. She probably came with David, don't you agree?"

"Yes," Patrick said. "But to dope her and leave her here like this—wait till I get my hands on that—"

"Stop. Try not to think of what might have happened," Colin said. We've got to get our evidence. Our villain's going to lie low pretending not to know what's happened here. The whole village will be in a state of shock anyway, after the murder of Mrs. Bradshaw. You came down to see Ellen but as you could get no answer you thought the cottage must be empty. Then you found the fire, but you still didn't suspect that anyone was here. You'll have to stay here—I'll get these two away before the fire brigade arrives—and for God's sake keep your temper."

As he spoke they could hear the fire engine's bell as it raced towards the village along the main road. Pretty quick, Patrick thought, bundling Ellen into Colin's car. She was able to sit up now and murmur, and the other victim was stirring too, and groaning.

"If our villain makes no move tonight we'll pay a call in the morning," Colin said, getting into the car. "They'll be expecting some enquiries after the discovery of two charred corpses in the cottage. Keep your head Patrick, these two will be all right, I'll have them at the hospital in no time, and I'll get back as soon as I've sorted out the local boys."

He drove off, and had just cleared the end of the lane when the fire engine turned into it. Eleven minutes had passed since Patrick had telephoned.

He could do nothing for Ellen. He thought then of the books, still stacked along the walls of the sitting-room. There might be time to save them.

A fireman climbed a ladder to the thatch, and with an immense pair of wire-cutters tackled the wire netting which covered the roof of the cottage. It had rotted through and rusted in many places, and soon some of the men were tearing it away, then raking down the burning straw in great bundles which lay smoking on the ground, to be soused with water from their hoses. Two more fire engines arrived, more hoses were run out, and as water poured on to the building searchlights were rigged up to light the scene. Patrick carried armfuls of books to his car, and the firemen worked on. Suddenly, as they tore a great hole in the centre of the thatch in an attempt to confine the blaze to one end of the roof, the whole thing went up in a burst of flame, like a very successful bonfire. It would be a miracle if even the shell of the cottage were saved, Patrick thought, plodding on.

He noticed, almost absent-mindedly, Cicero's *Orations*, the blue Oxford edition, as he carried them out, and as he laid them in his car he saw that volume five was there, restored to its proper place among the others. He got all the books out, and most of the furniture from the sitting-room, helped by Fred Brown who had seen the flames from the pub and come to lend a hand. They stacked chairs and tables on the lawn.

Before they left the cottage for the last time, Patrick, standing in the kitchen, looked for anything else of value, and saw a coffee pot with the dregs of coffee still inside it, on the stove. On the drainer, washed and standing upside down to dry, were three cups and saucers and three spoons.

Something struck Patrick as odd about this, but he could not pinpoint what it was. He glanced round again. The sugar bowl was on the dresser, and beside it was a book. It was volume five of Cicero's *Orations*. A second copy.

III

Patrick and Colin spent what was left of the night in the spare room at the Meldsmead Arms. The firemen eventually stopped Fred Brown and Patrick from entering the cottage again because the ceiling might fall in. They had raked the whole roof free of straw; it lay in sodden, smoking heaps around the cottage, which looked like a stage set in the beams from the searchlights; paper peeled from the walls, and upstairs the wrecked bedroom furniture was heaped anyhow in the two rooms as the men trampled back and forth with their hoses. A few charred rafters speared upwards into the sky.

"Looks like a bomb's hit it," muttered Fred. "Glad the old lady never saw it. Pitiful, isn't it?"

And it was: the burnt, frayed remnants of the curtains hung sodden in the window frames, water poured from every crevice, and above all was the acrid smell of the smouldering straw.

The lane was blocked solidly by fire engines, and at least one of them would be remaining throughout the night in case the blaze broke out again. Patrick's car was hemmed in by them. He locked it, and left it there, filled with the books. As an afterthought, he removed from its place in the set volume five of Cicero's *Orations*. It fell open in his hand, and out dropped an envelope. It was addressed in neat copper-plate *To Miss Ellen Brinton or Whomever Else it May Concern*, and had been opened, but the letter it contained was there. Patrick took it and the two copies of the book back to the pub. A police guard was set up at the end of the lane where it joined the main road, and, belatedly, a second guard was placed at the church. Colin brought Patrick's coat back from the hospital. He had left Ellen, half-conscious, muttering something about a letter, and was relieved when Patrick produced the one he had found in the Cicero.

"Sensible girl. She put the book back in the one place where no one would think of looking for it: its proper one," he said. He showed Colin the second copy, and told him about the three cups and saucers, the spoons and the coffee-pot. "They'll still be there in the morning, unless the firemen knock the whole lot over," he added. "The kitchen wasn't touched by the fire. But they're tramping in and out all the time and pouring water everywhere. The coffee-pot wasn't washed."

"There won't be anything in it. The cups were washed because two were doped," said Colin. "Those two were loaded with barbiturate."

"That's what I thought," said Patrick. "It shouldn't be difficult to trace the sale of this second copy of the *Orations*. It must have been quite recent. Our case is building up."

"Yes. If we can only get that final link in the morning," said Colin. He had spent hours with the local Chief Constable and on the telephone to his own Superintendent, but after he and Patrick had read the letter written by Miss Forrest and concealed in the Cicero, he rang them both again, before he and Patrick at last went to bed.

In the morning, a telephone call to the hospital brought news that both the patients were improving. This made it possible for Patrick to enjoy the splendid breakfast provided by Fred Brown's daughter, as he and Colin sat down to plates of two fried eggs each, crisp rashers of bacon, tomatoes and fried bread, and a huge pot of tea.

Then they set forth on foot. The single fire tender outside Mulberry Cottage took up most of the narrow lane; past it, towards Abbot's Lodge, Patrick's car was pulled in tight against the fence. In the morning light the cottage was a sad sight; the mounds of straw on the ground around it still smoked, and the air was full of its smell. The scene that had made Patrick think of a stage set in its unreal light the night before was now like a ruined doll's house. He could see a broken chair in an upper room; the bed from which he had snatched Ellen was on its side, charred. Through the middle of the building the chimney rose up, gaunt, unsupported by any roof on either side. A fireman walked about up there, picking up bits and pieces that lay strewn around, then throwing them down, uncertain what to do about these vestiges of human occupation.

"The fire people's forensic boys will be over sharpish this morning," Colin said. "No one was saying much last night, but I think they've a shrewd idea of how it began."

The rescued furniture stood about the garden in a forlorn fashion, looking like job lots waiting for an auction and damp with dew, though saved from the deluge of the firemen's hoses.

"We should have found something to cover them with," said Patrick, regarding the collection glumly.

"They've been saved. A bit of polish will soon put them right," said Colin, in a housewifely way. "People's effects always look pitiful after anything like this. When you go through pockets and handbags after accidents and list the contents, they're always pathetic."

"Haven't you got used to it yet?"

"Only up to a point," said Colin wryly. "Come on. There will be plenty of time to sort all this out later, and we'll make some arrangements for storing them. The forensic chaps may want to look at them. At least it's going to be another fine day."

It was true. The cloud that had filled the sky earlier was already drifting away. They walked on down the lane and through the gates of Abbot's Lodge. One of the garages was closed. Outside the other stood Carol's car, parked on the concrete wash. They walked up to the front door and rang the bell.

Carol Bruce opened the door. She wore slacks and a

sweater, which showed her figure to be slim and boyish. On both the other occasions when Patrick had met her, she had worn a dress. His final doubt about how everything had been managed disappeared.

She looked at them both enquiringly.

"I'm sorry to disturb you so early, Mrs. Bruce," said Patrick. "This is Inspector Smithers." For the time being they had decided to suppress Colin's connection with the C.I.D. and drop the Detective part of his rank.

"Oh? What can I do for you, Inspector? If it's about that dreadful accident in the church yesterday, I can't help you. I was in London all day, as I've already told the police."

"It's not about that, Madam." Colin put on his most official manner. "It's about last night's fire at Mulberry Cottage. Do you know where we can find Miss Valerie Brinton? Dr. Grant thought you might know her address and telephone number."

"Yes, I do. But what's all this about a fire, Inspector," Carol asked him in surprise.

"Didn't you hear the noise in the night, Mrs. Bruce? The fire engine bells. Of course, you are rather tucked away down here and the wind was blowing the other way."

"I heard nothing, but my room's at the far side of the house," Carol said. "I went to bed early last night—soon after the police left. I was upset about Madge, and I haven't been sleeping well since my dog died. I took some nembutal."

"Mulberry Cottage has been almost burnt out," said Patrick.

"You said you had Miss Brinton's address. May we come in while you write it down for us?" Colin asked, stepping over the threshold as he spoke.

"Of course," said Carol. "How terrible about the cottage. What a good thing it was empty. It's destroyed, then."

"Very seriously damaged," Colin said. "It must have been burning for some time before it was discovered."

"Did your husband hear nothing either?" Patrick asked.

"He didn't come home last night," Carol said. "He sometimes spends the night in London."

She led the way through the hall into the large, beautifully furnished drawing-room. Colin's gaze went swiftly to the bookshelf in the corner by the fireplace; then to the Sheraton writing-desk between the two long windows overlooking the garden. Carol was walking towards it. She picked up a narrow-necked vase that stood on its top, tipped it up, and a key fell into her hand. Then she opened the desk and took out a leather-bound book, turning the pages until she came to Valerie's address. She wrote this down on a piece of paper, followed by the telephone number, and gave it to Colin, replacing the address-book in a pigeon-hole inside the desk. Both men saw that everything was very neatly arranged there, with no loose papers about. Each compartment held its allotted contents.

"Use my telephone, if you wish," Carol said. "Is the fire still burning?"

"Smouldering," Colin said.

"Poor Valerie. What a shock for her. And I don't suppose she's heard about Madge yet, either. Two tragedies in a day."

"Let's hope there'll be no third," said Patrick, watching her.

"Of course, one always fears fire, with thatch," Carol was continuing.

"Oh, I don't know," said Colin. "Many a thatched cottage has stood for centuries. But once it catches, it's hard to stop it."

"The telephone's over here," Carol said, leading him towards a table in the corner of the room. Colin consulted the paper in his hand, dialled and waited. There was no reply.

"She must be out. Was she planning to come down here?" he asked.

"I've no idea," said Carol. Her expression hardened.

"You could have got her number from Directory Enquiries," she said.

Her manner had subtly altered, and Colin's did too.

"Mrs. Bruce, where did you and your husband spend your summer holiday?" he asked, and there was a steely note in his voice.

"I don't see what business it is of yours, Inspector, but we had no holiday this year," Carol said. "We were involved with buying this house in September, and we had no time nor any money to spare."

"I mentioned no particular month, Mrs. Bruce," said Colin. "Yet I believe you were in Greece this September, weren't you?" He had moved so that he stood between her and the open desk, and Patrick was now in front of the bookshelves. "I noticed a passport in your desk when you got your address book out just now. Do you mind if I look at it?" Colin asked, and before she could stop him he took it out of a pigeon-hole and turned the pages. It was stamped clearly by the Greek authorities and showed she had arrived at Athens airport a week before Miss Amelia Brinton died, and left on the day following her death.

"I—I had to go to Mykonos for a few days, to write an article about a painter who lives there," Carol said. "My husband was away on business then, himself."

Was he indeed? thought Patrick grimly. Ellen had been away too, when her great-aunt died.

But Colin was continuing smoothly.

"You spent some time in Athens," he stated.

"I flew in there, yes. Then I went on by boat, from Piraeus."

"You visited the archaeological sites in Athens, I think," said Patrick. "And you took your Benn's *Blue Guide of Athens and Environs* with you." He reached up and took the volume he had named from the shelf beside him. "I think you'll find page 29 is missing." He handed the book to Colin who opened it and confirmed this fact. Patrick then took out his wallet, and from it removed the page he had found, weeks before, on the hill of the Acropolis of Athens.

"What a coincidence," he said. "I found this page near the spot where Miss Amelia Brinton was standing before she fell to her death down the steps of the Acropolis. She was pushed," he added, looking up and surveying Carol in the manner in which he habitually addressed his students, "by what looked like a youth, hurrying by." He handed Colin the piece of paper, and the policeman placed it in the book. It had been unevenly torn, and the paper matched.

"It fits," cried Colin, like Dandini with the glass slipper.

"My discovery of this piece of paper was witnessed by the Greek police," Patrick went on. "And a photostat copy was made. There were prints on it."

Carol was staring at them. She seemed stunned and her expression was dazed. She had spoken the truth when she said she had taken nembutal, Patrick realised. She wanted to be found genuinely asleep, if anyone had come to arouse her. Besides, all along she had acted out her fantasies, even to the extent of making herself sick with laburnum seeds which could have killed her, since it was difficult to say how many would be fatal. A grisly form of Russian roulette. He pressed on.

"You were dressed in jeans, and you wore a wig that made you look like a long-haired youth," he said. "I expect we'll find it somewhere in this house. You've used it again, haven't you? You followed Miss Brinton for days, knowing that she would go up to the Acropolis, or to one of the other sites, looking for a chance to jostle her and make her fall. You may have tried before, or failed because she didn't stand in a suitable place, or there were too many people about. You knew that at her age she might not need to fall far; shock and a few broken bones would probably prove fatal. But she broke her neck, and she could never say that someone had pushed her."

Carol still seemed transfixed. Soon she would start to

recover, protest, defend herself. Patrick's voice went remorselessly on.

"You wore your disguise again when you killed Miss Forrest," he said. "You knew she had recognised you when you found a bunch of flowers outside your house and realised, as you soon did after you met Valerie Brinton, that they had come from the garden of Mulberry Cottage. You heard in the village that Miss Forrest had been staying there. And then you remembered signing a copy of Cicero's *Orations*, volume five, when you were a pupil at Slade House. So you looked for the book. You didn't want anyone to remember Clarissa Daniels."

At this, Carol did start slightly. Colin nodded to Patrick to go on.

"The girls of Slade House School gave Miss Brinton an Oxford edition of Cicero, unaware that she already owned the Teubner. All the volumes were signed by the donors. You couldn't find the incriminating volume because, after she recognised you, Miss Forrest took it away. You followed her as you'd followed Miss Brinton, looking for a chance to push her in front of a bus or a train, perhaps. In fact, you chose stairs again. You knew her heart was weak. No one noticed you in the British Museum in your disguise. They're used to long-haired youths."

At last Carol spoke.

"You must be mad!" she cried. "Inspector, I don't have to listen to this! Why should I kill two harmless old ladies?"

"They weren't harmless where Clarissa Daniels was concerned. They knew about her career at Slade House, and that she'd been in prison later," Patrick said.

"We've traced your record, Mrs. Bruce," Colin said.

"So you've been in prison, have you, Carol?" said a voice from the doorway. "What else have I to learn about you?"

All three of them turned at this interruption. David,

very pale, with a bandage round his head, stood looking at them.

"David! But you're—" Carol's voice trailed off.

"Dead, you thought. Well, I'm not, despite your efforts, and nor is Ellen," David said. He advanced into the room, his eyes fixed on his wife's face. "I worked that part out in the night. You killed Madge, God knows why, and you meant to kill Ellen and me. I've come to see that you don't get away with it."

He looked at Colin, and a dim memory of the night before came to him.

"You're a policeman, aren't you?" he said. "Well, then, you'd better know that my wife's car was parked in the lane beyond the village, near the church, yesterday afternoon. I came back that way with Ellen. Most people come to the village by the other road. I suppose she was up in the belfry then, waiting for Madge. Why Madge?"

Carol took a step towards him.

"I'm not afraid of you now, Carol," he said. "I suppose you came back by the main road later. By then I'd put the car away and locked it up, and I was at Mulberry Cottage with Ellen. I didn't care any more. I'd decided to leave you." He looked at her with loathing. "You didn't have to kill us. I'd have given you plenty of money, just to be rid of you."

He stopped and looked at Colin.

"I've been in the hall, listening. Did she really kill Miss Brinton and Miss Forrest?" he asked.

"We have reasons to believe she may have been concerned, yes," said Colin, the cautious policeman. "Please go on about last night, Mr. Bruce. What happened at the cottage?"

"We—Ellen and I—didn't know about Madge—not till this morning. The cottage must have seemed empty to the police—we heard knocking, but we didn't pay any attention."

The implications of this were not lost on Patrick, but after all, he had known it already. He concentrated on what the other man was saying. Clearly, David Bruce did not yet know the full story of all Carol had done.

"Ellen and I decided to have it out with Carol last night," he told the other two men. "We asked her to come down for coffee and said we wanted to talk to her. She must have doped our coffee. She did it very cleverly, and she must have given us a lot of the stuff, we went off very quickly. We'd scarcely begun our discussion."

Carol spoke at last, and her voice was high.

"You're mad, David. I can see you've had some sort of accident, and it's affected your mind."

"It's brought me to my senses, you mean," said David. "I was mad when I married you." He swayed slightly and reached out his hand for support. Colin went to him, and Patrick's attention wavered from Carol. It gave her her chance. She rushed past them all through the door, and banged it behind her.

"She won't get far," said Colin. "Are you all right?"

"Yes—sorry—I just felt a bit dizzy. I've been clonked on the head rather hard. Carol, I suppose." He said it without surprise.

"How did you get out of the hospital?" Colin asked disapprovingly. There had been no police guard on him or Ellen; it hadn't seemed necessary.

"Slipped out when no one was looking," said David, with a sheepish air. "I came in a taxi." Then he looked grave. "I had to come and attend to this business. You realise that after Ellen and I passed out she carried Ellen upstairs and undressed her? I suppose I was too heavy for her, she must have meant to roast us side by side."

They all heard, then, the sound of Carol's car outside, and Patrick made a move for the door.

"No—don't stop her," David said. A most extraordinary look came over his face. "One other thing she and Valerie had in common, they both drive bloody fast," he added.

They heard the sound of the Lancia roaring into the lane; they heard the screaming brakes. Alone of them all, Carol did not know that a fire-engine blocked the way outside Mulberry Cottage. Going much too fast to stop, she pulled over to squeeze past it, not caring if she ripped the wing of her car against the hedge. Almost in the ditch, scraping by, she saw a red mini coming towards her.

Because there was one person in her life whom she genuinely loved, Carol pulled over still more to the side. She missed the mini, but her own car left the road and burst into the field beyond, bounced over once, and struck a tree.

IV

She was still conscious when they took her out of the wreckage of the car, but she died before the ambulance arrived, without uttering a word. All that she did was to look at David with an expression of contempt on her face, and then turn her head to where Valerie was standing. The other woman, quite unhurt, dropped on to her knees beside Carol and took her hand; Carol smiled at her, then she closed her eyes and it was over.

It was Colin who took off his coat and covered the body. Patrick's mind flew back to Athens and that other body on the steps of the Acropolis, with which it had all begun, and he felt a sort of pity until he thought of Ellen and how nearly she had been another victim.

"What has been going on?" asked Valerie. She seemed perfectly composed, just very pale. "I heard that Madge Bradshaw is dead—and David, you've hurt your head." She frowned at him. "Why was Carol dashing off like that? And the cottage—"

She knew nothing. Someone would have to tell her the whole story, beginning in Athens. Or need they?

Patrick, suddenly feeling a great weariness, looked at Colin.

"If you'd just tell me where I can find you during the day, Miss Brinton," the policeman was saying. "You've friends in the village, I expect, where you could go? Your niece is quite all right, just a bit shocked by the fire."

"Ellen was here? In the cottage?"

"Yes, but she's all right," Colin repeated.

In the end, Patrick took Valerie to the Kent's house, where she agreed to remain until the police said she might leave the village. As he left, she was springing into action, demanding to telephone first the hospital about Ellen and then her insurance company.

Would-be sightseers, coming to gaze at the scene of the fire, found the end of the lane cordoned off by the police, and news of Carol's fatal accident soon travelled round the village. This would sound the final knell for the reputation of Abbot's Lodge, thought Patrick grimly, and wished that it, too, might burn down.

Later, when he had finished with the local police, Colin took him up to the belfry in the church so that he could see the small trap through which Carol had dropped a great stone on Madge's head as she passed below. The stone had been found in a pile of mowings in the churchyard. Silently, Colin pointed to the roster in the church which declared that Winifred Kent was due to arrange the flowers that weekend.

Madge wore a scarf over her head, so Carol didn't recognise her," he said.

"But—it was Friday—don't people do the flowers the day before?" Patrick asked. "On Saturday?"

"Winifred told her other guests, on Thursday, after you'd all left, that she'd be doing them the next afternoon as she and George were going out for the day today. Of course, they cancelled that, after what happened. Oh, and she'd mentioned, too, that she was at Slade House."

"And Madge was bringing back the brass she'd cleaned," Patrick said slowly.

"Yes," agreed Colin. "The vicar said she did this once a month or so. The unknown factor, where Carol was concerned."

Lionel Merry had been shattered at what had happened in his church and knew he would never forget the terrible scene he had found, with Madge, her head battered in, lying in a pool of her own blood, and the candlestick that had killed her on the ground nearby, bearing traces of her hair and bits of bone.

"The ironical part is that Winifred doesn't remember Clarissa Daniels," Colin went on. "She said she's a lot older than Clarissa—Carol—and they can't have overlapped at all, at school."

After their visit to the church, Patrick and Colin went to the Kent's house, where Valerie was told she might leave. She sped off at once in her mini to Sussex, where it seemed she had a painter friend with whom she often stayed, but remembered before going to thank Patrick for saving the books and so much of the furniture.

Winifred could still scarcely take in the fact that Carol had intended to kill her, not Madge.

"Even if I had recognised her, would it have been so terrible," she asked. "What had she done that was so awful? We aren't all judged by what we did at school, I hope."

"She'd lied and cheated—cribbed at exams, and stolen money," Patrick said. "And other girls were blamed at first, for she was clever." All this had been revealed in Mildred Forrest's letter. "Eventually she was expelled."

"Did she kill Mildred too?" asked Winifred, and from their silence knew the answer.

"But why? Did they meet in Meldsmead? I thought Mildred left before the Bruces moved in?"

"They overlapped by a day," said Patrick. "Mildred went to Abbot's Lodge with some flowers. She saw Carol through the window and recognised her at once. She was arguing with David. Then the lights went out. Mildred rushed off, dropping the flowers in the drive. Carol must have found them later and realised she'd been seen, and what was worse, recognised."

Mildred had said that the lights at Mulberry Cottage worked that evening. Perhaps Carol had arranged the failure at Abbot's Lodge as another omen.

"But she wouldn't know who'd called," Winifred persisted.

"She'd have known from the village grapevine, or from David who'd have heard from Ellen, that Mildred was at the cottage," said Colin.

"And she'd recognise Amelia's prize chrysanthemums," said George. "I expect that's what Mildred took. Carol would see them at Mulberry Cottage—she and Valerie were friendly right away. They were thick as thieves, in fact, even though Valerie has this painter woman down in Sussex."

"Oh, darling!" Winifred protested.

"It's true," George said. "For the last few weeks, whenever Bruce has spent the night in town, Valerie's been here at the cottage."

"Oh, poor Valerie," breathed Winifred. "Carol was out of her mind, of course."

"Poor Valerie, yes, but don't waste your pity on Carol," George said grimly, taking her hand. He thought of what he might have lost, and of what had happened to Denis Bradshaw who was now at the vicarage in a state of shock. "Think of her victims."

Patrick remembered all this as he drove to the hospital later on with a bunch of roses for Ellen. If only he had acted more quickly, or realised sooner who Carol was, or thought of looking in that vase for the key of the desk, Madge might have been saved. Instead of concentrating wholly on the problem, he had let his mind wander into thoughts of dalliance with Ellen. All along, he had known there was a puzzling factor about Miss Brinton's fall. She had dropped down a short precipice, rolled across a sort of landing and then down a steep flight of steps. If she had simply lost her balance she would have remained on the landing, though at her age such a fall might, indeed, have proved fatal. But she had fallen outwards, in a trajectory, well across the landing, rolling over it and then down the stairs. She had received a fairly hearty push to gather so much impetus, just as Miss Forrest, in the British Museum, had not crumpled up but had rolled some distance.

Another time, he vowed, if he came upon a chain of incidents that made him scent disaster nothing should deflect him from his course; no other woman should ever interfere with the workings of his brain.

But meanwhile, there was Ellen.

She was not in her bed in the hospital. She was visiting David, who had been taken back and put to bed after the events of the early morning. Patrick saw them together through the glass window in the door of David's private room. Ellen, in a dressing-gown much too large for her and looking very pale, was sitting in an armchair by his bed. David was asleep, and Ellen watched him; on her face was the same expression Jane's wore when she looked at her small son Andrew.

"It's not right. That's not the right emotion," Patrick seethed inside himself. But he could not fight it. He looked down at the flowers in his hand. What a useless gesture! Well, someone would like them. He saw a passing nurse.

"Here, nurse. Give these to some old lady who hasn't any flowers," he gabbled. "Or keep them for yourself. The person I brought them for doesn't need them now." He pressed them into her surprised arms and rushed away, leaving the nurse staring after him, amazed. She took them to the nurses' home, for the wards were all as bright as Chelsea Flower Show, and told her friends she'd been given them by someone who had brought them for a patient who had died.

V

Patrick looked at his watch. He could be back in Oxford in time to dine in hall. The prospect filled him with gloom. Then he remembered that Jane and Michael knew nothing about all that had just happened. He went back into the hospital, found a telephone, rang them up to ask if he might come over, and was urged to do so.

Jane was putting Andrew to bed when he arrived at North Crowley. Michael gave him a large whisky, and when he had taken a mouthful of it, suggested a walk round the garden.

"The dahlias are still blooming," he said. "It's getting dark, but you can just see them in the dusk."

The two walked round the garden twice, along neatly mown paths which separated the roses from Jane's herbaceous border, without talking.

After a while, Michael said: "Gardens are rather soothing. I dug up what seemed like half an acre while Andrew was being born. Decorating's good, too. I did out the cloakroom when Jane had that last miscarriage. The dining-room's next."

"Tell me when you're going to start," said Patrick. "I'll give you a hand."

He managed a smile, and Michael knew the cure had begun.

"Let's finish our drinks, and stack up new ones," he said. "Jane will be down any minute."

She found them seated in silence, one on each side of the fire, where some logs were burning. Her mental radar told her instantly that Patrick was sad and Michael concerned.

She had to know.

"Is Ellen all right?" she asked.

"Oh yes," said Patrick. "Perfectly."

"That's good, then," Jane said, and waited. When the silence continued, she added, "There was a little in the paper about Madge—just a few lines. I suppose there will be more tomorrow."

"Carol killed her," Patrick said. He told them then the story of the past hours, and they listened without interrupting till he reached the end.

"If I'd only thought of looking on the backs of the photographs for the names," he said. "Or if I'd found the key of Carol's desk in that vase when I was at Abbot's Lodge that night. Then I'd have seen her passport and been sure about Athens."

"The name Clarissa Daniels wouldn't have meant a thing," said Jane. "She changed it, I suppose. She must have been paranoiac—why commit murder because you meet someone who knows you've been a cheat at school?"

"There was more to it than that," Patrick said. "She'd been to prison for embezzlement—she'd been working in an insurance office and helped herself to some of the funds. She wrote to Amelia for a character reference before the trial, and the old girl wouldn't give it."

"I'm not surprised," said Jane.

"That isn't all. Later, she was in business with some woman, running a shop of some sort. They couldn't make a go of it, so they set the place alight, to get the insurance money. Odd how people run to type. She lied and cheated all her life, and went in for arson more than once."

"What about the other woman—the fellow-arsonist? Did they both go to gaol?"

"Oh yes."

"Was she blackmailing Carol, then? Threatening to expose her?"

"No. She died. Fell down the escalator at Green Park, late at night," said Patrick. "It was just before Carol married David. No one saw it happen."

There was a silence.

"Was David the one with the money, then? You thought it might be Carol."

"Yes, it was David. He inherited a fortune from his father, and the controlling share in a family business."

"So that was why she married him."

"Yes. She had expensive tastes."

"What about the book? The missing Cicero? Why was that significant?" Jane asked. "Ellen put it back with all the other books, you said."

Patrick had forgotten the books. He had stacked them in the parish hall, along with Miss Brinton's rescued furniture, but he had forgotten his promise to sell them. Now there would be no cosy weekends with Ellen, picking out the volumes one by one.

"You asked about the Cicero," he said, aloud. "Mildred recognised Carol through the windows. She remembered that Amelia had been given the two sets of Cicero, the *Letters* and the *Orations*, by the school, in a fit of generosity. Because she kept her Teubners away from her pupils, they thought she had no Cicero. Each volume was signed by the girls who gave it, and Carol —Clarissa—was among those who signed volume five of the *Orations*. Mildred thought the book might be important, so she took it. Perhaps she thought as she'd remembered it, Carol might too. It seems that Amelia had mentioned Carol just before she went to Greece —wondering if she'd taken a grip on herself. So it was all fresh in Mildred's mind."

"Fancy her writing it all down!" said Jane.

"It was lucky she did. We'd have a lot of gaps that we'd be guessing at, otherwise," said Patrick. But they would still have known about Carol. Her record would have been discovered.

"And Carol thought if she replaced the book, you and Ellen would stop fussing. Why did she bother, if she meant to burn the place down?"

"She didn't at first. That was a last-minute plan, when David and Ellen told her they wanted to get married."

He found he could say it quite easily, to his surprise. "Up till then, she hadn't meant to kill Ellen." At least, he thought not. David was the one who would have a fatal accident, devised to make it look as though he had intended it for Carol.

"I don't understand what David saw in Carol," Jane said. "Why did he marry her?"

"He's—he's not a very strong character," Patrick said. He had been going to say that David was definitely weak, but he modified it. "Carol was very capable. That was what drew him." And now Ellen's quiet efficiency had the same effect.

"But the dog? Why go so far? And the laburnum seeds?"

"It was all real to Carol," Patrick said. "She acted out her fantasies. At first probably she was just looking for an isolated country house where she could plot unobserved. Then, when she heard of Abbot's Lodge and its reputation, it played into her hands. She made it look as though the house was continuing to harm those who lived there. The police think she filled the dog with sleeping pills—I expect they'll dig him up now, and have a look. She probably ate a few laburnum seeds herself—enough to make her symptoms authentic. She'd asked David to buy the pie, to make it seem as if he'd added them."

"What if he'd eaten some?"

"He doesn't like blackberry-and-apple, it appears," said Patrick.

"How subtle," Jane said, and shivered. "But she really cared for Valerie?"

"Oh yes. She saved her life. She'd got past my car—it was pulled in well to the side—but the fire engine blocked the road. She scraped past it, half in the hedge, going very fast, and then saw Valerie in front of her. She pulled into the field to miss her." He remembered the look on David's face as they heard Carol's car start. The taxi that had brought him from the hospital had dropped him on the further side of the fire engine. He knew

Carol would go fast down the lane; he wanted her to crash. Wouldn't that memory haunt him and Ellen for ever?

"How did Carol start the fire?" asked Michael.

"With paraffin. There was a ladder in the shed. The forensic people thought she'd soaked rags and shoved them into the thatch on the windward side of the cottage. The straw was very dry underneath; once it caught, it was just like a bonfire."

"And Mildred wanted to see Ellen that day in the British Museum to warn her who Carol was?"

"Yes. She said so in the letter she left. She seemed to have a premonition that she might die without telling anyone, hence the letter."

"Which Ellen read only yesterday?"

"Yes. And she didn't tell David what it said. I suppose she wanted to spare him," said Patrick.

"Carol was a devil, wasn't she?" Jane said. "One of Miss Brinton's failures. I suppose nowadays a child like that would be psychoanalysed. Would that have cured her, I wonder?"

"Who can tell?" said Patrick. "There was one other thing."

"Yes?"

"Madge Bradshaw was very ill. She'd got to have an operation—it was critical. Denis knew, but she didn't. I don't know if that makes it better, or even worse."

The others were silent. After a while Jane spoke.

"Nor do I," she said.

"She wouldn't have died violently, nor so soon, if I hadn't been so thick-witted," Patrick said.

"There'll be a post-mortem, won't there? That will show just how ill she was," Michael said.

"Yes. But to die like that—her head—" Patrick's voice trailed off. He had seen the photographs of Madge's body. Perhaps she had felt only the first blow, when the stone hit her. But perhaps she had seen and recognised her assailant, before death came.

"How did David hurt his head?" asked Jane. "Did Carol bash him too?"

"Yes. She couldn't lug him upstairs. He thinks he may have moved around, but he doesn't remember. She clobbered him with the door-stop," Patrick said.

"Those books," Jane said. "Valerie's. What's going to happen about them now? You won't want to cope."

"I don't know," said Patrick. "Thornton's would love to deal with them, I'm sure."

"You'd better write to Valerie and suggest it, then," said Jane. "The sooner you unload that chore the better."

"On the principle of plucking out the offending member. Yes," said Patrick. "I agree."

"That's settled then," said Jane briskly. She would never meet Ellen now. "Oh, and stay the night, Patrick," she went on. "Michael's doing a little painting job tomorrow, and he'd like some help. He's going to do the baby's room."

Michael gaped at her.

"Am I?" he asked, and earned a glare.

"So soon?" said Patrick. "You mean to be prepared."

"I bought the paint this afternoon," said Jane.

"I see you share your husband's views on therapy," said Patrick. He got up and looked out of the window. It was quite dark now. "Very well, dear sister. You've just hired yourself a painter."

ABOUT THE AUTHOR

MARGARET YORKE was born in Surrey, England, and now lives in a Buckinghamshire village. She published her first novel in 1957 and has since written numerous crime and suspense works, which have been published in almost a dozen countries. She was the 1979–1980 Chairman of the Crime Writers' Association. She is also the author of *Cast for Death* and *Dead in the Morning*.